I0742812

Also by DJ Geribo

Novels
The Mart

Short Story Collections
Deep Lake House
Seven Storied Houses
Ten Storied Buildings

Non-Fiction
Me & Them
The Miracle Dog

Children's Books
Mouse Bound
Eddie Easel and the Case of the Missing Green
The House at the Top of the Trees

Both the publisher and the author encourage you to purchase directly from www.BBDPublishing.com as this supports the author in the most direct manner.

You can also ask for many of the author's works directly from your favorite bookseller.

Select titles are available on Amazon in paperback and Kindle formats.

USEFUL PIECES

USEFUL PIECES

DJ Geribo

BBD Publishing ~ Alton, NH

Useful Pieces is published by

BBD Publishing
P.O. Box 351
Alton, NH 03809

www.BBDPublishing.com

Book Layout and Editing by James J. Fontaine

Cover Design by Positively Creative Solutions, LLC

Printed in the United States of America

10 9 8 7 6 5 4 3 2 1

Library of Congress Control Number: 2025942608

ISBN 978-0-9883068-9-9

TABLE OF CONTENTS

Chapter 1

Sean stepped out onto the front porch. Fall was coming; you could always smell it in the air first, especially at night when the warm days cooled a little. He inhaled deeply, filling his lungs with the leaf-crisp air. He loved that smell. Decaying leaves he supposed it was; an earthy smell that he couldn't get enough of. He hoped it wasn't laced with mold; he could always smell mold in food products. Jill laughed at this because he would open a package of rotten chicken and think it smelled fine. But throw a little mold in there and he wouldn't touch it. So, salmonella ok, mold not ok. Of course, he knew neither was good but he guessed his paranoia about mold had something to do with his having read too much about it and how it can make you sick. Some molds, if grown in the right conditions, can produce mycotoxins that are poisonous, the worst of which are aflatoxins that can cause cancer. So, yeah, call him paranoid but he had done his research and wanted to steer clear of anything that had the slightest chance of having mold on it.

The yard around the property had lots of deciduous trees which would make for a colorful fall landscape. Since it was only the beginning of September, they still had a few weeks to wait before the full spectrum would appear. Sean walked to the edge of their property and looked up at the mansion looming over him. The stone behemoth cast a dark shadow over the modest carriage house, guest house is what the realtor had called it, where he and Jill now lived. Although it was also the

Charmeins' property, he felt like it was theirs while they were renting even though they'd just moved in a mere two weeks ago, barely enough time to feel settled or any real sense of ownership. He looked up at the manor again and felt it staring back in judgment. He refused to let his new landlords' house intimidate him and slowly, to make his point, turned his back to the dwelling and walked, head held high, back to the guest house, not once looking over his shoulder. He wouldn't give it the satisfaction.

Inside Jill was in full-throttle makeover mode. Painting the walls was a simple fix that Sean had agreed with. Not much else had to be done to the place, even though it hadn't been rented out, according to the realtor, for at least a couple of years. Obviously, it had been maintained by someone, otherwise there would have been more repairs needed, both indoors and out. He was thankful that he didn't have to spend his already limited time fixing broken door locks and rotted window sills instead of on his writing and running his own bookstore. He was actually pretty good at home maintenance since he'd grown up with a dad who could do all that and Sean had learned from watching. But he preferred not to have to do it. He would much rather spend his days writing. Sometimes he regretted opening a bookstore since it took a lot of time away from his own writing. But he needed to make some money and with Jill's job teaching while also building her business as a fine artist, the two of them were out straight and had little time to fix or repair their new place. Still, in a way, this new place was a dream come true and a mini-mansion of sorts with its stone fireplaces and arched doorways. Although it was only five rooms, a couple of them were big and since Jill needed more room for her studio, she took the larger of the two largest rooms with the other being their bedroom. He was fine with the smallest room since he only needed space for his desk with his computer and printer and a couple of book shelves and preferred having his own space rather than working in either the kitchen or living room.

"Need some help?" Sean was more interested in pouring a glass of wine and sitting on the front porch than picking up a paint brush and getting hot and sweaty. This September was feeling more like early August and without A/C to cool the place and no sign of a cool breeze making an appearance any time soon, he thought it was a better idea to put off painting the walls until it actually started feeling like fall. He always had more energy in the cooler months. Even his writing suffered during the summer. He had considered purchasing a window unit. Maybe next summer.

"No, I've just finished this wall and it's time for a break. It's too damn hot. What's for supper?"

"I'm thinking liquid. What do you think?"

"Sounds good to me." Sean poured them both a glass of chardonnay and they walked out to the front porch which conveniently had two wicker rockers complete with padded seats and backs.

Sitting on the porch they both sighed and after relaxing for a moment, turned their gaze to the mansion frowning down at them. Jill stood up to get a closer look.

"Is it just me or does the mansion appear to be looking down at us, almost like it's judging us? Or maybe it's just judging the house we are living in. Maybe it doesn't care about us at all. Or am I being weird?"

Sean laughed. "Funny, I was thinking the same thing just a few minutes ago. It does have a certain air about it. It definitely seems to have a personality. So not weird. It's either that or maybe both of us are weird."

"Or maybe it reflects the people inside. I mean, we really don't know anything about them, except that they are stinking rich. Maybe they had this guest house built for that reason, to look down on the peons who rent it. You know, look at us, we're so rich and you aren't."

"Do you really think people who have lots of money think like that and would actually build a guest house, for their 'guests', just so that they could look down on them? I don't know, I think wealthy people have more important things to think about. Sounds petty to me. Let's not judge them and maybe they won't judge us. Or at least let's wait until we meet them. Which, by the way, is this Sunday. Remember?"

"Yes, I do. So, what do you bring people who have everything?" Jill didn't like going empty-handed when someone had invited you to dinner. She thought that was rude. Even if they said, 'Just bring yourselves,' you should bring flowers or at least a bottle of wine.

"Ah, nothing?" Sean chuckled at Jill's raised eyebrows and stern mouth.

"No, I think we should bring a bottle of wine. And maybe we can get them drunk and then they'll tell us how they came to be so wealthy. You know, share their secrets."

"Well, the invitation did say 'dinner and drinks' so I'm guessing they at least drink alcohol. Sounds like a plan, my dear. Here's to us." They clinked glasses and, sighing, settled deeper into the fluffy seat cushions.

Chapter 2

Your presence is requested at the home of
Noah and Charlotte Charmein.
The occasion: Dinner and drinks
Date: Sunday, September 22
Time: 6:30pm
Dinner will be served promptly at 7pm
after drinks and hors d'oeuvres in the parlor.
Dessert and coffee will follow dinner
after a short rest in the parlor.
We request that you arrive on time.

The invitation seemed much too formal for dinner with their new landlords. It was more like a wedding invitation than an invitation to come to dinner. Jill wondered if they should dress formal – she didn't think she had anything that fancy to wear, except maybe her wedding dress. She did have skirts and blouses so hoped that would be dressy enough. She was starting to sweat and it was only 4:30. She couldn't understand why she was so nervous. She tried to imagine what the Charmeins were like. Stuffy and snobby? Or condescending? Maybe sweet and tolerant? Or perhaps just a touch of 'I'm better than you and I know it.' Jill wasn't exactly sure why she thought of them using these words. She had never met anyone as wealthy before and really had no idea what they would be like. Maybe she saw too many TV shows that portrayed the wealthy as being superficial and self-important. But deep down she knew they somehow weren't like her and most likely didn't think like she did either.

"So, are you about ready?" Sean was wearing khakis and a polo shirt. He looked like he was ready to go play nine holes of golf.

"Really? That's what you're wearing?"

"Yeah, really. Why, what should I wear? A suit and tie? Not happening. This is 'dinner with the landlords', babe. I'm not going to try to make any kind of an impression. If they don't like me for who I am then we won't have much of a relationship with them. Which I'm thinking is probably how this landlord/tenant thing will go anyway. It's kind of the same thing as boss/employee. So probably best to keep it casual and not get too involved with each other, you know?"

"Well, I guess we can see. They might decide to take us under their wings and support our arts. You never know. Maybe we can play up the whole 'starving artists' thing. Although they probably already know that about us. I'm sure they know much more about us than we know about them. What do we know about them anyway?"

"Just what the realtor told us. They have no family – never had children. And I guess all of their other relatives are dead. Who knows, maybe they're looking for someone to take over the house and all of their assets. Ha! Wouldn't that be grand? How old are they anyway?"

"Sean, don't get any evil ideas. They are our landlords, that's it. And how would I know how old they are? So, anything else about them?"

"Not much, um, I think Cheryl said something about them being filthy rich but we've already figured that out. I've been wondering why they'd want to rent this place out. Maybe just to keep it up so it doesn't get run down. Cheryl thinks they're just a lonely old couple and enjoy having young people around. They certainly don't need the money." Sean checked his reflection in the mirror and straightened an invisible tie. Smiling, Jill shook her head and touched up her lipstick.

"That seems obvious. Maybe we should go into town and see if anyone can tell us anything more."

"You mean the town that is ten miles away? I would guess they don't get out much. So, people who live in the area probably don't know much about them."

"Hmm, what an odd couple. I really am curious how they made their money, though. Maybe it is old money, from back in the day when people like J.P. Morgan or the Vanderbilts were around. Didn't they make money in shipbuilding? Or was it the railroad?"

Sean loved it when Jill asked questions he knew the answers to and rattled off the facts as if taken right out of Wikipedia.

"Cornelius Vanderbilt was a shipping and railroad tycoon, a multi-millionaire and one of the richest people in the 19th century. Interesting to note, his father was a farmer and boatman and Cornelius quit school at age 11 to work on the waterfront."

"Oh, like Marlon Brando in "On the Waterfront", he 'coulda' been a contender'?"

"That was a movie my dear, these are true facts."

"Ok, smarty pants, what else?"

"Well, he was quite ambitious and bought his first boat when he was sixteen that he used to ferry people from New York City to Staten Island. That led to a fleet of boats that were used during the war of 1812. There's a lot more. Are you bored yet?"

"You are a wealth of knowledge. And no, I'm not bored, yet."

"You do remember that I'm an author and research is just part of what I do when I write. Facts, just the facts. The internet is full of them and weeding out the real from the fake is yet another task I'm burdened with when I write a novel."

"Ok, Captain Obvious, I'm well aware of what you do. No need to explain. I'm just messing with you."

Sean smiled knowing that his wife did this often enough that he really shouldn't have to explain. But it was all part of their friendly banter, which was part of what made their relationship so strong.

They arrived at the massive front doors to the mansion up the hill from where they were living. They stood in awe of the mansion for what seemed like twenty minutes but they knew it couldn't have been more than a couple, both in their own worlds, admiring the stone work, the gardens near the front door, and the overall architecture of the place that towered over their humble abode. They turned to each other and then to the front door where they'd just rung the door bell, expecting a butler or some other servant to open the oversized solid double doors. When a gentleman in a smoking jacket and black trousers opened the door, they were sure it had to be Mr. Charmein himself.

"And you must be the Porters. Sean and Jill, correct?" The doorman, aka Mr. Charmein, extended a hand to Sean and then Jill, stepping aside from the door allowing them entrance to the great hall.

"Please, come in, won't you?" Mr. Charmein closed the door behind them and then ushered them down a long hall, heading toward what they imagined would be the parlor.

"You are right on time. I do like it when people are punctual. I think it is rather rude when you invite someone to your home and give them a specific time and they arrive when they find it convenient for them. And you wait, wondering if they are even coming while the meal gets cold. Do you agree?"

Jill gave Sean a side glance and was about to whisper her response when Mr. Charmein turned to them, waiting for a response.

"Oh, yes, of course, very rude." Jill caught herself and turned sympathetic eyes to Mr. Charmein.

Sean thought he should also acknowledge his agreement with Mr. Charmein. "I agree as well, very rude, sir."

"Oh please, call me Noah. And this is my lovely wife, my darling Charlotte. I do sometimes call her Charley, a pet name."

A woman, looking more like a doll than a real person, she couldn't have been much more than five feet tall, got up from her chair and, holding what Jill guessed was a glass of champagne, extended a white-gloved hand.

"My love, these are our new tenants, Sean and Jane."

"No, it's Jill." Jill couldn't believe that in just a few seconds he had forgotten her name.

"Oh, how very nice to meet you." She barely touched their hands with her gloved one and then promptly sat back down.

"Sit, sit. Would you like some champagne? I just love champagne and welcome any opportunity to imbibe. It is the most lively drink, the bubbles are just fabulous, you know." Charlotte continued to sip.

Sean and Jill looked at each other and both nodded, feeling for just a second like a pair of bobblehead dolls.

"Champagne, yes, great. Um, we also brought this bottle of wine for you both to enjoy some other time."

"Oh, well, that was sweet. Noah, take the bottle please." Noah, who was sitting on the sofa next to Charley, after filling glasses for Sean and Jill bounced up and took the bottle into the kitchen. Jill had a fleeting image of Noah dumping it right into the trash. She made a mental note to bring champagne the next time if there was a next time.

"So, are you both enjoying the cottage? I think everything had recently been repaired, it just needed some fresh paint which I believe you are both taking care of, correct?"

"Oh yes, we've been painting the inside. It's a lovely place, the cottage, yes, lovely. Thank you for leasing it to us." Sean continued nodding agreement and had to force himself to stop.

"Well, we really have nothing to do with who lives there. As long as you answer the questions honestly and your references check out, the realtor handles everything. She selects who lives there and so far it has worked out fine." Charley stopped to take a sip. Not sure if she was finished talking, Jill and Sean waited.

Noah had returned and sat looking at the couple and Charley looked around the room. Jill and Sean stole a glance at each other and took sips of their champagne, wondering where they should go with the conversation.

"How long have you lived here and how long have you leased your cottage?" Sean decided to jump right in with the questions. He was never comfortable with quiet for very long.

Noah and Charley laughed at the same time, both sipping their champagne before answering. Sean thought maybe each was waiting for the other to answer.

"Well, let me see now. We've lived here, oh, I guess since we were about your age, in your early thirties I'm guessing?" Noah took a sip from his champagne before continuing.

Sean nodded agreement.

"Yes, well, time sure does seem to fly by, doesn't it Charley?"

Charley seemed mesmerized by her champagne and stared into her glass at the bubbles rising from the bottom and popping at the top.

Since Noah didn't seem to have anything to add to the single statement he'd made, Sean reminded him of the second part of his question.

"And you've been renting the cottage out the entire time?"

"Oh, sort of. People come and go, you know. Many want their own home or children. Oh yes, you aren't planning on having children any time soon, are you?"

Jill looked at Sean. They both seemed to think that was a rather personal question and felt like it was a job interview from the 1950's when women weren't hired if they were married since the employer assumed they would be having children and leaving the company. But since they'd talked about this and were waiting until they bought a house before starting a family, Sean saw no harm in answering.

"No, not now, not for a while. Like your other tenants, we also want to buy a house before we have children. And we aren't even sure if we'll have any at all. We're both committed to our careers."

This information seemed to perk up Charley. Jill, on the other hand, thought Sean was sharing too much and threw him a glance.

"Oh, careers, how exciting. And what are your careers, if I may ask?"

Charlotte said 'careers' like she was whispering the name of royalty, breathless and hushed.

Since Sean had done all the talking thus far, he nodded to Jill to go first.

"Well, I'm an artist. I paint very large-scale paintings. Kind of abstract, you might say. But I do have a theme. Mostly it is chaos which is a lot of the way I see the world. I also work at the elementary school as an art teacher. It's a lot of fun but takes a lot of energy, too."

"I see. Painting and then painting with children. Do you like working with children?" Charley raised her glass to Noah so he could see she needed a refill. He quickly got up and topped off her glass. Sean wondered if she typically drank this much or if she needed it to get through meeting the new tenants.

"As I said, it can be tiring since they have so much energy. I really wish I didn't have to work there and could just do what I love, which is paint. I will be having a show soon, though. It's in Madison, a few towns away. I do wish you would come to it."

Noah and Charley exchanged a look, both with raised eyebrows, and then both started to laugh. Jill and Sean also exchanged a look that intimated the Charmeins were exactly as they'd thought; most likely eccentric and quite possibly mad, as well.

"What's so funny?" Sean couldn't resist.

"Oh, dear, don't worry, we aren't laughing at you. It's just that we never go anywhere, not two, three, ten, or even one town away. You see, we are so happy to live in our home and we enjoy each other's company so much that we never leave the house. People really can be a bother and over the years it seems we have both developed, ah, what is it called now, oh yes, agoraphobia." Noah seemed pleased that he had remembered the name of the affliction that had apparently struck both he and his wife.

"Interesting, both you and your wife have agoraphobia?" Jill asked suspiciously.

"Yes, well, you see we have both been indoors for so many years now so yes, we both have this condition." Noah dumped the rest of his champagne down his throat, quite sure that was the end of that conversation.

"But what do you do for food, social entertainment, or everyday necessities like toilet paper, soap, laundry detergent, that sort of thing." Jill just couldn't fathom living this kind of existence and had a whole new perspective of the wealthy owners.

"As I said, dear, if you had been listening, we enjoy each other's company. As for food and all that other stuff, the necessities you mentioned, well, that's why we rent out the cottage." Noah poured more champagne into his glass and, again, topped off Charley's glass. Sean and Jill had each only taken a sip or two and now found themselves intrigued by where their conversation had turned, hanging on every word either Noah or Charley said.

Jill was slightly confused and didn't make the connection immediately.

"I don't get it, what does renting the cottage out..."

"We're their gophers, Jill. We'll be running their errands. Isn't that right, Noah?" Sean had figured it out in an instant and looked at Jill, now glaring at the Charmeins who were looking at each other, smiling, raising their glasses and drinking the bubbly.

Noah responded by toasting Sean and then Jill. "Now, why don't we go eat some dinner. We're having roast chicken and potatoes with asparagus. Unless of course you don't eat chicken then I'm afraid you will be going home hungry."

Noah put his arm out for Charley who stood up, wobbled a little, and then leaning on Noah, walked together slowly into the dining room. Sean and Jill exchanged hard stares while Jill shook her head from disbelief over what had just transpired between them and their new landlords.

The dining room was – as would be expected in a mansion – elaborate, expansive, and ornate. Noah sat at the head of the table with Charley to his right. Plates were set to Noah's left where Jill and Sean were seated. The meal was laid out on the table which made them both wonder if there was a maid or at least a cook who prepared their meals. Sean was going all out and after that revealing cocktail hour, decided he had nothing to lose.

"So, you have a cook?"

"What makes you ask that?" Noah seemed genuinely surprised by the question.

"Oh, I thought you were completely alone here. Sorry, my mistake."

Noah laughed. "No, we do not have a cook. We made all the food ourselves. We both enjoy cooking. Kind of a hobby for us. We try lots of different dishes, adding all kinds of herbs, spices, and other things, you know?"

"But we were in the parlor for an hour and everything looks hot like it just came out of the oven." Sean and Jill both noticed how wonderful it all smelled, too.

"Well, yes, there is this new invention, I think it is called a chafing dish? As you see, each chafing dish has a flame underneath it to keep the food hot. We didn't want to disturb our visit by cooking. That is so rude. Don't you think? I think it is better to prepare the meal in advance and keep it warm until you are ready to eat." Charley was quite animated while giving this explanation.

Chafing dish, a new invention? Jill smiled but nodded agreement. Mostly she was agreeing that it certainly was obvious that they didn't get out since they didn't seem to know about modern conveniences. It was like they were living in the 1800's.

"Do you have internet access here?" Now she was deliberately messing with them. Sean looked at her surprised as he took a bite of his chicken.

"Do we have what, dear?" Noah wasn't acting, they could tell. He really didn't know what Jill was talking about.

"You know, the internet, for email or surfing the web? Do you have computers? Or how about cable TV?" Noah and Charlotte both put their forks down and stared blankly at their guests.

Noah started laughing. "Oh yes, yes, I do remember our last tenants had talked about the 'internet' and 'computers' or something like that. It has been at least a year or so since we last had tenants, though. I guess things change so fast nowadays."

"So, how have you been getting your food and other things if you haven't had tenants to do it for you?"

"Well, we do have a gardener and a housekeeper who picks things up for us at the grocer's, too, occasionally. The gardener is here once a month and the housekeeper is here every other week. We give her a list and money and she does a little cleaning, too. We do prefer to have tenants but haven't found any suitable for quite some time. So, we are very happy to have you here."

Noah stopped suddenly and glanced at Charlotte who looked at him reprovingly. He put his head down and concentrated on his food.

The table was quiet for a while; only the sounds of silverware cutting up chicken and their muted chewing with mouths closed could be heard. Sean had another piece of the baked chicken and Jill took a few more of the asparagus spears. When they had finished, after they'd all put their forks down and blotted their mouths, they continued sipping the wine that Noah had opened for dinner.

"This meal was delicious. And the wine was a perfect complement. Thank you so much." Jill was trying her best to forget the unspoken deal that had been made between landlord and tenant. Her time was precious to her and now she was going to have to run errands and shop not only for her and Sean but for these two oddities as well. She wasn't exactly thrilled with this new arrangement.

Noah stood up from the table and pulling Charley's chair out, again offered her his arm to walk out of the great dining room. It seemed as if, just for a second, they'd forgotten about their company. Sean and Jill took the cue and also stood up, following the couple out of the room.

"We aren't much for dessert but I believe we have some chocolate chip cookies if you'd like." It was obvious that the visit was over. Sean and Jill graciously declined and they all headed for the front door.

"So, we'll see you tomorrow for the list of errands we will need you to do for us. Any time after you get home from work. And what time is that again?" Jill knew they had not discussed what time either she or Sean normally got home from work.

"I get home around 6pm, usually, sometimes earlier, sometimes later. Several nights a week Sean isn't home until after 9pm. So, it won't be until later."

"Hm, well, that won't do. We'll have to figure something else out. Perhaps you could come by before you leave for work? Or maybe you'll just have to come by on the weekend. Are you both around then?"

"I usually am, but sometimes Sean has to work." She was getting a little annoyed by Noah's attitude. She was feeling more and more like hired help, but without getting paid, of course.

"I'm sure we'll get it all worked out eventually. But for now, let's just concentrate on getting here tomorrow morning."

"I have to leave the house by 7am to get to school on time."

"That's fine, then come by at 6:30 – we won't take too much of your time. We just need to go over a few things with you, get you accustomed to our needs and our routines. We'll see you then." And, after seeing them out, Noah gently shut the door behind them.

Jill walked briskly to the guest house at the bottom of the hill. Sean had to walk faster than usual just to keep up.

"I thought it was dinner and dessert with coffee? Did they seem like they wanted to get rid of us? Hey, what's the rush? It's still early and a beautiful night."

"Didn't you hear, I'm on duty tomorrow morning at 6:30 – I have to get to bed so that I'm NOT FUCKING LATE to start working for our landlords FOR FUCKING FREE!" She hoped the Charmeins heard at least a few of her choice words.

"Yeah, I hear ya. A little rude, don't you think?"

Jill stopped abruptly and turned to face Sean. "Rude doesn't even come close to describing how the Charmeins behaved tonight. I mean, just like that we are unpaid labor for them? What are they thinking? I don't have time for this. Do you? Seriously Sean, I'm not doing this."

"But you just told them you'd come by in the morning. And now you're telling me that you're not?"

"I told them no such thing. I told them what time I had to be to work. If you think this is so much fun, why don't you do it? Why did he just focus on me? Because I'm the woman? I'm the one who runs errands? The 'little woman' of the house? I didn't see Charley jumping up and tending to their guests, did you? This is definitely not going to work for me." Jill continued down the path to their rental, fuming all the way.

Chapter 3

The night passed quietly between them and continued into the morning. Jill was up and out of the house before Sean woke up. He slept on the couch because he'd gotten the feeling that was what Jill wanted even though he was confused about what he'd done wrong. Sean hadn't picked her to do the errands. But he also realized that he hadn't done much to stand up for her. Truth be told, he was glad Noah didn't focus the errand-running on him. He decided he needed to do a little more investigating into the Charmeins' personalities and livelihood. He also realized he never did get an answer to his most important question: where did they get the money to afford such an elaborate and ostentatious mansion? Perhaps it was in the family and they simply inherited it? They had seemed evasive to Sean, were always able to somehow put the attention back on Sean and Jill and take it off of themselves. It also seemed that when Noah shared too much, Charley had been quick to change the subject.

Since it was unclear to Sean if Jill really was blowing off the Charmeins and hadn't gone to their house this morning, he decided he should go to pick up whatever errand list they had. Sean arrived at the Charmeins' door at 6:42. As soon as he knocked, the door swung open and he was greeted by Noah.

"Good morning, my dear. I'm sorry to see you are a little late…" Noah stopped in the middle of his sentence and nearly gasped when he saw Sean standing in front of him instead of Jill.

"What are you doing here?" Sean was taken aback a bit since it hadn't been obvious to him that they wanted only Jill to run their errands. He felt they should be grateful that he and Jill were doing their errands, no matter which of them came by to get their list.

"Jill couldn't make it, so you get me."

"Well, I didn't expect you to just make that kind of decision without telling us first."

"Oh, well, it wasn't clear to either Jill or myself that you only wanted Jill to do your errands. That really won't work for us because she is very busy and sometimes might not be able to get here as early as you'd like because she needs to be in school early and it'd be just too much for her to get here and then get to school on time. And since her job is more important, well, that will take priority over coming here for your list first thing in the morning. Since I don't have to be at work until around 9am, I will probably be the one coming here in the morning for your list. We'll both do your errands, but for today, and probably most mornings, this works better for us."

"I see." Noah stared at Sean for what seemed like several minutes. Sean was getting uncomfortable and was just about to break the silence when Noah quickly handed him the list and just as quickly closed the door.

"Well, I love you, too. What the fuck?" He shoved the list into his pocket and left.

Sean had a little time before work so decided to head to Webster, the town that was the closest to them, and see if they had a library that had a computer he could use to try to find out something about the Charmeins. Or maybe there were people in town who knew them. He decided to go to the town hall first to find out if they were actually considered residents and if they paid taxes. Someone surely must know about them and have some information about who they are and where they came from.

He walked into the town clerk's office and talked to a woman named Peggy as the name plate on her desk stated. Just Peggy, no last name. I guess in a town so small you only need to know a person's first name.

"Do you have information about all the residents in the town?"

"What kind of information are you looking for? We don't really give out information about the residents if that's what you're looking for."

"Well, what about the sales of homes? You do have that kind of information, correct? And isn't that information available to the public? What about taxes that are paid on a home each year, is that available? Also, do you have a list of all the residents, which would be the people who pay taxes, and is that available to the public?"

Peggy's eyes started to narrow as she looked Sean up and down.

"What exactly are you looking for, young man?"

"I'm a writer and I'm doing a little research. We are renting the cottage that the Charmeins own. I was wondering if you could tell me anything about them."

"The who? We have a lot of residents in Webster and I don't know all of them."

"Really, a lot of people in this sleepy little town? That is surprising."

Again, Peggy narrowed her eyes at Sean and folded her arms across her ample chest. He thought it best not to piss off the woman who may be able to help him find the information about the Charmeins that he was looking for.

"I'm sorry. I'm sure you are very busy and have a lot of people to take care of in this town. I didn't mean to be rude."

Peggy unfolded her arms and taking a pen, started to write on a pad of note paper.

"How do you spell that name?"

"Charmein, c-h-a-r-m-e-i-n. They are both in their 70's, I believe, live in a mansion, huge house, beautiful, must have been built in the early 1900's or maybe before."

"In this town?"

"Yes, about 10 miles away, or so."

"Hmm, don't know of any mansion. Are you sure?"

"Yes, I'm positive, we were in it last night. And they are the owners of the place we are currently living in."

"Well it must be a new place. When did you say it was built?"

"Yeah, it is not a new place. It was built in the early 1900's, I said, I think. So, it is strange that you have no information about it. Are you new here?"

Peggy gave him a dead-eye stare.

"I've worked here since I graduated from high school some 30 years ago now, young man. There was a time when I knew everyone in this town. Of course, the town has grown. But a mansion? I have never heard of it."

Peggy continued to look for the name Charmein.

"Sorry, I have no record. Maybe in the archives."

Sean started to settle in and wait for the next search but decided to leave and start his own search.

"No, that's fine. You know, we actually may be part of the next town over so, thank you for your time."

"Like I had nothing else to do."

"You have a nice day, Peggy." And Sean walked out the front door. What was it about town employees, he wondered, that gave them this attitude like you were somehow interrupting them whenever you asked them a question. Weren't they 'town' employees, meaning that they worked for the people of the town? He noticed the same situation with our 'elected' senators and reps. When did they become the elite where we aren't supposed to bother them with our problems? Aren't they working for us? Didn't we hire them? Don't we pay their salaries? How is it they have the best of everything while everyone else struggles to make ends meet? Did we decide that the elected officials should have more and better than us? How did they get to be so damn special? This thinking always irritated him, so he brought his thoughts back to the task at hand; trying to find out what he could about the Charmeins.

He decided to check out the local library. There was usually a town history section and, if he was lucky, the librarian may even have been around when the Charmeins' house had been built. He smiled at the thought and pictured a relic with cobwebs hanging from her arms and woven through her hair. When she opened her mouth the standard, barely audible phrase came out "Can I help you?" He was still smiling when he opened the door of the library and was greeted by a 30-something young woman behind the desk. She smiled at Sean which caused him to blush at his own inaccurate account of who would be standing behind the desk of the modest and charming library.

"Can I help you?" At least he was right about the soft-spoken voice. The sign on the desk said "Marsha Owen, Head Librarian."

"Well, maybe, um, Marsha?" She nodded agreement. "I'm wondering if you have a section on the town history, you know, things like, who lived here, the homes that were built, anyone famous for example?"

"Oh sure, we are a small library but we do have a section dedicated to local history in our history section.

Here, let me show you. You could also search on the computer, but you probably already know that. And if you can't find the book you are looking for, we do have interlibrary lending available." Sean followed the young lady to the back of the library. Although it was only two rooms, they did seem to have a good variety of books available.

"Yeah, I know about that, but since we don't seem to have the internet out in the sticks where I live, I guess I'll have to be coming in to town to use your computer when I want to look something up. Unless we can get the internet out where we are. We just moved here and don't quite have everything set up yet."

"And where might that be?" Sean found himself walking closer to the head librarian than he normally would but he really couldn't hear what she was saying. Maybe she had worked at the library so long her voice just didn't project any louder after several years of whispering.

"Oh, um, about 10 miles out. At the Charmeins' mansion – we're renting the cottage guest house."

"Hmm, I'm not familiar with that house."

"I've heard that before. Sounds like it is the town's best kept secret."

"Ok, well, here we are. If I can help you with anything else, just let me know. My name is Marsha, as you now know. But Barb and Christine can help you, too. Oh, and if you want to use the computer, you just have to sign up for it. You can use it for about an hour at a time, sometimes longer if no one else is waiting. And we often don't have anyone waiting. Except on Saturdays, it gets busier on the weekends."

"Great, thanks for your help."

Sean grabbed several books off the shelf and brought them back to a table, which happened to be the only table in the adult section of the library. A sign on the wall pointed to the children's section downstairs. He flipped through the books and found very little about the town of Webster. Although this was the closest town to where they lived, he was beginning to think that they were actually part of Lebron, the next town in the opposite direction that was about seventeen miles away. The realtor had told them the house was in Webster but maybe somewhere along the way the boundaries got changed and now they were a part of Lebron. He should have found out that information at the town hall. But since Peggy was so busy and unwilling to give him more than five minutes of her time, he had to figure out another way to get that information. Maybe one of the realtors in town could help.

He decided that was enough research for one day and he would take a trip to Lebron another time. Right now, he needed to get to the bookstore.

Chapter 4

When Sean got home, he delivered the groceries to the Charmeins first. Again, he got the cold shoulder from Noah who quickly took the packages. Sean gave him the change, and after checking the receipt, Noah just as quickly shut the door. Shaking his head at the rudeness of his new landlord, Sean walked into the cottage and found Jill had locked the door to her studio. He knew they had to talk about this situation. This couldn't go on; he knew he had to take on some of the burden of catering to the landlords.

"Jill, can you come out and talk to me." He banged and couldn't keep the anger out of his voice.

She preferred to listen to classical music when she painted. Today she was listening to Queen. He could only assume she was either not painting or she was in an aggressive painting mood. This was usually when she was getting rid of tension or anger. Something similar ended up on the canvas. To Sean, this was a waste of good canvas. Her usual style was strong, surreal, but also organic. He loved her work. But Queen or AC/DC usually turned her canvases into something similar to what Jackson Pollock produced. He knew a lot of artists would argue with him and would extol the genius of Pollock. But that was why he was a writer and not a painter. He didn't get the fascination with what he saw as the work of a 3-year-old.

Jill cranked up the music a little louder. Sean felt his blood pressure rising along with anger. But he had been learning about the dangers of anger and allowing it to control your life. He wasn't going to let that happen to him. He took a few deep breaths and tried again, different approach.

"Jill, I love you. I will do whatever you want but I can't bear to be separated from you this way. I need you."

The music stopped and within a few seconds, Jill opened the door and stepped out into Sean's arms.

"I love you, too, babe." They hugged and as they stood there wrapped in each other's arms, they each felt the anger melt away.

"So, what are we going to do? What can I do to make this work for all of us? Obviously the Charmeins had this in mind when they decided to rent this place. I'm sure this is what they always do, which is why their tenants move out and find their own place. But, you know we couldn't have found such a nice place with such a low rent. This was a rare find. So, it would be great if we could make it work. But we have to do this together. Can we make this work? What do you think?" Sean was a pro at summing up situations.

"Yes, we can. I agree. I like it here, it is such a unique place and it has everything we need. It's comfortable and cozy. But yes, we have to do this together. We have to work out a schedule."

"A schedule sounds doable. If the morning is too early for you, then I'll take it. I don't have to be in as early as you do, you shouldn't have to feel stressed about this first thing in the morning. And I can probably do a few errands before I have to be at the bookstore. Today I did them on my way home since they gave me a grocery list. I guess it depends on what the Charmeins need us to do."

"But I got the feeling they wanted me to be their gopher. What do you think they'll say if you continue to show up? Which reminds me, what happened this morning? Were they surprised to see you?"

"You could say he was surprised. It was like I was a little errand boy. Noah handed me a list without barely a word spoken and not even a thank you." Sean shook his head reliving Noah's rudeness. "Well, they are going to have to come up to the twenty-first century and deal with me, like it or not. You are not their personal hausfrau. If they can't accept our deal then I guess we could look for another place. This is nice, but it isn't worth it if it is going to cause tension between us. Agreed?"

Jill smiled and planted a huge kiss on Sean's lips. The kiss, as it often did, led to the bedroom.

♟ ♙

The days passed quickly and the fall colors intensified. Leaves began to fall and winds to blow signaling the next season rolling into the area. Jill was inspired and spent as much time as possible in the studio. Although Sean was the one who had more time to cater to the Charmeins' needs, it seemed to be working out for both of them. At least he wasn't complaining about it. Jill wondered how long that would last, though.

Jill was in the living room enjoying a crackling fire in the fireplace and sipping a glass of Chardonnay. Not at all unusual, except that it was 10:30pm on a school night. The bookstore had an author event so had stayed open a little later than usual and Sean, along with the guest author and a couple of the store clerks, hung out after discussing the event, which was a success. Jill was usually in bed no later than 10pm since she had to get up at 5am. Sean decided to proceed with caution.

"Hi, Hon. How are you doing?" As he approached the couch where Jill was curled up in as close to the fetal position as she could get with a glass of wine in one hand, he saw the tissues, lots of them, on the floor right beneath where she sat.

She didn't answer and instead fresh new tears began to spill out of her eyes. Her eye makeup was long gone. In sync with her eyes, her nose also started to run. She grabbed another tissue and as she started to blow, Sean noticed the wine glass in danger of spilling onto Jill and the couch so took it gently from her hand and placed it on a table, a distance away where it was safe from being knocked over. And that was all she needed. She burst out crying, loud sobs, as Sean wrapped his arms around her and squeezed in next to her on the couch.

Jill cried until she couldn't possibly have any more tears in her. Sean waited for her to get it all out so that she could tell him the source of her pain.

"They're letting me go."

"Who, the school?"

"Yes, the school. A teacher who was on maternity leave came back. They promised her she could come back when she was ready."

"Wait, but you weren't a temp until someone on maternity leave came back. You were replacing someone, permanently, or however long you wanted, right? Isn't that what they told you back when they first hired you?"

"That's right, that's what they told me. This is someone who used to work for them and didn't think she wanted to come back to work after she had her baby. But her baby is about two now, she's probably bored, and she changed her mind. And I don't have a contract so they can just throw me away." Tears spilled over and down her cheeks again. Sean held her tight.

"What the hell! We should be able to sue them!"

"Sean, I don't have a contract with them, remember? They were going to give me one but I guess I was on probation until they were sure they wanted me. Apparently, I just didn't work out."

"Don't be ridiculous, you're a fabulous teacher. I've seen you with those kids, they love you." Sean remembered the day he stopped in to bring Jill her lunch that she'd forgotten on the kitchen table. The kids were all giggly and polite, raising their hands to ask Jill who Sean was and asking Sean his name and if he was Jill's husband. Several of them wanted to touch his velour jacket and one even patted his sneaker. Of course, they were in art class so a few of them were already covered in paint, fortunately water-soluble. The paint on Sean's white sneaker had come off easily.

"Yeah, but the kids don't make the decisions. They probably loved the teacher who is coming back, too."

"Look, you'll find something else. And there are other schools around."

"Sure, just add a half hour onto my ride. Do you realize we are living in the middle of nowhere?"

"I know, maybe we should think about moving, find something that has more opportunities for both of us. Near a city, or at least a suburb that isn't so remote."

"We did that, remember? We've been doing that. We've lived in cities, near cities, in suburbs and we both decided this was the quality of life we wanted. I can't possibly go back to living in a city or even near a city. And a suburb is usually just too family-oriented with kids running around and there is too much chaos, kind of like the city except with more trees. We just didn't fit in. And then there is your bookstore, you commuted over an hour each way for several months, remember, and now we are only ten miles from it so you have more time to write, too. We can't give that up. You can't give that up. Maybe this is the opportunity I need to just put everything into my art and take some trips to New York and try to get into some galleries there."

"Or maybe we can find a nice retirement community." Sean smiled, hoping to break the line of negative thinking Jill was following. Although he was impressed that she was thinking 'New York galleries', something he had mentioned many times before.

"Very funny, I'm not ready for that yet. As it is, I feel like we are living in a retirement community right now with our neighbors, Noah and Charley."

"Ha, you're right! But seriously, babe, let's think about this. We'll check the papers and see what's in there first. I'll ask around, I meet a lot of people in the bookstore. I can check the town hall, they could use a new clerk."

"Did they say they were looking for one?"

"Ha, no, it was just my personal observation. You know, town workers, not the friendliest."

"Damn, Sean, what are we going to do?" The tears were filling up her eyes again and Sean hugged her tightly as she put her head on his shoulder, nestling into his neck. He was just settling into a good body hug when she jumped up to retrieve her glass. She started pacing while sipping. She called this her 'brainstorming time' although she and Sean usually did it together. Whenever they had an issue they couldn't agree on or just didn't see enough options to satisfy either of them, they would throw out ideas with Jill pacing the floor while Sean sat with his laptop, getting the ideas down as fast as they threw them out. Jill was in that pose, restless, pacing, running a hand through her shoulder-length blonde hair while sipping her half-empty glass of wine. Sean wondered just how much she had drunk so far, particularly if she still had her job and needed to get up early.

"Wait, one question, before you start pumping out ideas. Did they give you a two-week notice or are you finished?" Sean thought two weeks would be reasonable but since she'd only been there a few months realized this was probably her last day. Also, the wine. Jill was too much of a professional to go to work with a hangover, which he was pretty sure is what she was working on. Especially since her clients were all five to ten-year-olds.

"No, no. No notice. Today was it. They even had a check ready for me, how about that? As for ideas, there aren't any right now. Except the one about going to New York. I didn't hear any comments about that." Jill was pretty sure Sean didn't want her traveling to New York, alone. He just couldn't go off and leave his store to travel with her, for support. In the past he left for a couple of days but this would be a two-week trip. Jill didn't even know if they could afford it. They had talked about it before they moved into the cottage house but she knew she still needed a few more pieces and had to get a tighter portfolio together. If she was taking this trip, she had to make it count and being fully prepared was the only way she would go.

Jill was right. Sean was avoiding the "New York Trip" subject. They had talked about it before. And it didn't end well. He was so protective of her; he knew she was very self-reliant but they weren't talking about her going to the beach for a couple of weeks. She remembered the way he described it: 'This was the big city, full of crazies, just waiting for a pretty woman walking alone'. She knew Sean was afraid for her. Jill knew living in this small town wouldn't get her the exposure she was hoping for;

she knew she needed to go to New York. But now they might not have the money. She also needed more inventory, particularly if she was hoping for a one-person show. Maybe just finish a couple more of her large-scale pieces and that would be enough. Losing the teaching job might have been the best thing that could have happened to her. She needed to put a more positive spin on it. After all, her plan wasn't to be a teacher her entire life. Her passion wasn't teaching, it was painting. Losing her job teaching was about the weekly salary. Not painting was about losing her soul. She had far more invested there.

"Can we not talk about that right now? I think we need to focus on finding you another job, maybe something closer to home. Or maybe you can come work for me?"

"Sean, I'm not putting all of our eggs in one basket. If anything happens to the store, we are both out. No, the best thing is for me to finish up the last two paintings I want for this show, get my portfolio completed, and take that trip to New York. I have got to do it. I have to know if I'm good enough."

"And where does the money come from for those two weeks that you'll be living in a motel in New York? And food, taxis, other expenses, etc., etc.? How can we afford that right now?"

"I've worked this out - I have money from the trust that was left me. My mom always supported my art, more than my dad ever did, so I'll borrow a couple thousand dollars, that should do it, and I'll get my name out there. And when these jobs come through, I'll put the money back because I want that for our savings. This could work, finally, for me. You know what my art means to me. I wish you would support me on this. I have to do this, once and for all. If I don't, I'll never know. Just think how you would feel if you never finished that book or contacted publishers to get your book in print. You told me you didn't want to self-publish so you have to send your novel to so many publishers and hope they take it. You have to do this for your sanity, right?"

"Yeah, but I don't have to go to New York to do that. I can send a copy of the manuscript through the internet. It's a little different."

It was Sean's turn to pace while Jill sat. He was too keyed up to sit. And he also didn't want to see the sadness in Jill's eyes. He knew this was her dream. And he knew he had to let her do it. As much as he hated the thought of her going to the city by herself, he had to let her go.

"I do support you, I always have and always will. You know that, right? So, maybe we can compromise a little. Maybe instead of two weeks you can go for just a week. You should be able to meet with several galleries in that time, right?" Jill was so excited that Sean was finally understanding her need that she jumped up off the couch and ran into his arms, kissing his face all over. Sean laughed and hugged her hard.

"I love you so much, babe." He didn't want to let her go. But he thought of the quote, 'If you love something let it go. If it comes back to you, it's yours. If it doesn't, it never was.' He always had the tiniest bit of doubt.

"Back at ya'." Jill was happy beyond belief and taking Sean's arms from around her, they danced around the room.

Chapter 5

The next couple of weeks proved to be busier than either of them could have anticipated. Jill was determined to finish the two large-scale paintings while also polishing up her bio to bring to New York. She had contacted a couple of art galleries and they promised to give her time when she arrived. One of them had heard about some of the awards she had won and was very interested in meeting with her. Although the other one had not heard of her, she knew the gallery scene was a close-knit family and just by asking around they would find out who she was. She also wanted to set up two other appointments for the week she would be there but was having trouble reaching the gallery owners. She was hoping to contact them in the next week before she traveled to the city.

Now that Jill was home, she wanted to take some of the burden off of Sean so she decided she needed to help with running the errands for the Charmeins. That would give her a break from her painting, too, which she did occasionally need. She was well-aware of the value in 'stepping away' from her work and coming back to it with fresh eyes.

On her first day home after losing her teaching job she felt like she could finally catch her breath. Although she loved the kids that she taught at the school, teaching was never her goal or dream job. Painting was and always had been her life's purpose. Teaching was the way for her to get to where she wanted to be, working as a full-time artist. That well-known quote ran through her head "Those who can, do. Those who can't, teach." She knew the value of teachers and never thought of it as an unimportant job, she just knew it wasn't for her. For some people that was their goal. For her, it was a means to an end.

After Sean left for the bookstore, she cleaned up the breakfast dishes and decided to walk up to the Charmeins' place to see what they needed. She'd barely rung the door's bell when it was flung open by Noah.

"Good morning my dear Jill, and how are you today?"

"What?" Jill was more than surprised at the greeting and also at a loss for words.

"Are you all rested? You must be relieved to be out of that school job you had, aren't you? I'm sure you'll be much happier at home, taking care of your man, and us, of course, too!" Noah handed her his shopping list with a purse that contained the money to pay for the items on his list. Although he hadn't given them money with their shopping lists at first, having waited until they'd returned with the receipts, apparently he was now trusting Sean and Jill and paid for the items up front, almost to the penny.

"And we'll see you when you get back. Oh, and now that you aren't working, please do try to get here earlier, say by no later than 8am." And without so much as a good-bye, the door was closed in her face.

Jill stood at the entrance way, unable to move while she listed in her head the short-comings of her landlord. Several words came to mind immediately: rude, brusque, demanding, opinionated, judging, chauvinist. There were more but she was too upset to let herself continue and left as quickly as the door had been shut in her face.

Walking back to the cottage, looking back over her shoulder several times as she walked, she hoped the expletives exploding in her mind were reaching the ears of the landlord, if only through telepathy. And then she stopped as Noah's words hit her right between the eyes. He said 'Jill' before he'd even opened the door. Either he was psychic or he knew she would be standing at the door. Somehow, he knew. Just like he knew she was no longer working at the school. For someone who was so out of touch with the world around them, how could he possibly know, already, that she had lost the teaching job? And what was this bullshit about 'taking care of her man' and also taking care of them, too? She stomped her feet and ran the rest of the way to the cottage, slamming the door as she went inside.

She kicked her shoes off and paced back and forth, fuming, livid, incensed with rage. She couldn't remember the last time she was so upset. And then she remembered; she was this upset just a few days ago when she lost the teaching job. What was going on? She felt like her world was falling apart. Sean, her rock. She picked up her cell phone and dialed the bookstore.

"Good morning, My Favorite Bookstore, can I help you?" Sean sounded so professional she almost didn't recognize his voice.

"Sean?"

"Hey, babe, how are you doing?"

"Not too good. You can't believe these people, Sean. I don't know if I can deal with them anymore."

Sean was a little confused, not sure exactly what people Jill was talking about but if he had to guess, it would be the Charmeins, so he went with that.

"So, Noah? Yeah, I guess it would be Noah since we don't see Charley all that much. What did he do now?"

"He knew I was at the door before he even opened it. That is the first thing."

"Well, they do seem to be a little psychic though, don't they? I mean there is something a little spooky about both of them, like maybe they're hiding bodies in their basement or something bizarre like that."

"Sean, I'm serious. It was Noah and not only that, he knew that I had lost my job. How could he know that, Sean?"

Sean felt like she was blaming him. Like he, for some reason, had run up the hill to the mansion and told them his wife was no longer employed. Maybe she did think that. Since she was now doing their errands, maybe she thought he had filled them in on what was going on in his and Jill's lives.

"Babe, I didn't tell them anything if that's what you're thinking. I don't ever talk to these people. Except when I have to when I pick up their list of errands. So, I hope you don't think that I told them anything about you and your job. But since you couldn't do their errands before and now you appeared at their door, maybe they just assumed that you had lost your job. Maybe it was just a wild guess and he happened to be right."

Jill was quiet for a moment; was Sean actually defending their crazy landlords? She couldn't believe even for a second that Sean thought it was an innocent wild guess by Noah that she had lost her job. And since he'd brought it up, she wondered if Sean actually had said something to them about her losing her job and that she would now be doing their errands. That's what actually made sense to her. All of her anger was now directed toward Sean and she couldn't get off the phone fast enough.

"I gotta go."

"Babe, wait, you're too upset, talk to me." But he was talking to a dead line.

Jill sat on the couch, fuming, and was about to rip up the errand list when she saw something on it that caught her eye. One of the items was morphine. She knew one of the main uses of morphine was managing severe pain often associated with cancer. Of course, it was used for other painful illnesses, too. It was also an opioid and could only be prescribed by a doctor. But when did the Charmeins ever go to a doctor? They never left the house so how could they get a prescription for morphine? So many questions and nothing was making sense to Jill. Nothing at all.

Of course, if she had to guess, it would be Charley who was on the morphine. When she thought about the way Charley acted, she had noticed that she seemed dizzy and didn't stand up much, letting Noah take care of her. Jill knew that those were a few of the side effects of morphine; lightheadedness, dizziness, drowsiness. She remembered what her grandmother went through when she had cancer and when she was really failing and had relied on morphine for the pain. She was tempted to call Sean back and tell him about this news but decided instead to go into town to do the errands.

At the pharmacy in town Jill waited while the assistants were busy so she could talk to the pharmacist directly. When he was available, she approached him.

"Good afternoon, can I help you?"

"Yes, I have a prescription to fill. I believe Mrs. Charmein is a regular customer."

"I'll check my file." And he started to walk away.

Jill reached out and touched his white, starched pharmacist's jacket. He stopped and looked down at her hand and then up at her face. He relaxed when he looked at her and smiled in an almost flirty way. Jill did that to men and often took advantage of how easy it was to get what she needed from a man with very little effort. She smiled back at the pharmacist and softened her voice to a whisper, conspiratorially, looking around before asking him her question.

"I was wondering, can you tell me what this medication is for, what is the illness that Mrs. Charmein has?" She shamelessly blinked her big blues at him and continued smiling, not flirty like he did, but in a more 'I know I shouldn't be asking you this but don't you think I'm adorable right now?' way. She hoped that would be enough to distract him and that he would write down the information she was looking for without another thought.

"Are you a relative?"

"Well, um, no, but kind of. I don't think she has any relatives so, in a way I am, I guess."

The pharmacist continued smiling but now it was more of a 'caught you' smile, he was on to her and was back to being his professional self.

"I am truly sorry but I can't give out that information. And if you were a relative, you would know what the patient is using the medicine for. I'll be right back with this." And he turned his back to her and walked away.

"I must be slipping." Jill was surprised at herself. That innocent smile worked on just about everyone, particularly men.

She finished the other errands around town and drove back home. When she got home, Sean's car was in front of the cottage. She ran in wondering if something was wrong. He didn't usually come home in the middle of the day. He was sitting on the sofa drinking a mug of tea.

"Hey, everything alright?" Jill stood waiting for an explanation. Sean put down his mug and standing up, walked up to Jill and put his arms around her.

"Sean, is everything ok?" Jill pulled back from him to look in his face.

"I don't want you to be upset. I'm sorry. I know it must have sounded like I was defending them but I really wasn't. I don't know what the fuck is going on with them, they are odd, that's all I can say. But if you think maybe they are somehow involved in you losing your job at the school, maybe we need to look into it. I thought about it on the drive home. I would be suspicious, too. You were right to question how he knew that it would be you at the door. That is odd." He sat back down on the couch and picked up his mug.

Jill sat beside him and put her arms around him.

"That's all I need. I need you to hear me and believe me. I was feeling like I'm the crazy one but I knew I wasn't being crazy. I knew I wasn't being paranoid either. There is something going on here. They are somehow involved, I just know it."

"So, do you have any ideas? I'm open, whatever you want to do."

"I think we just need to be aware of what we are telling them and if anything else happens, we'll just confront them. I don't know if, at this point, we can do anything else. But right now, I have to bring them their groceries and medicine. Oh, yeah, I almost called you back to tell you this; I had to go to the pharmacy to get medication for Charley."

"Medication? What kind of meds does she take? Not that this surprises me, she certainly acts like someone on some kind of drugs. There is something a little off with her."

"Morphine."

"Morphine? Huh, interesting. Isn't that what your grandmother was on?"

"Yes, she was, when her cancer got really bad. I wonder if Charley has some kind of cancer."

"That would explain a few things, but there are still a lot of questions. The more I thought about what you said on the phone the more I believe you are right. They somehow knew you had lost the teaching job. But how? Most people in town don't even know anything about them. They are like some kind of enigma, both of them. Funny, I was thinking of them as one thing, an enigma, but they are two different individuals. But it is as if they are one and the same strange enigma. Singular. Does that make sense?"

Jill was nodding her head while he explained this last part. It was as if they were two people living as one. Very odd.

"I know exactly what you mean. But now I have to bring them their groceries."

"Right, and if you're ok, I'm heading back to the store. And I'll see you tonight. I'm there late tonight, so eat without me."

"I suppose I can start making you a lunch to bring, since I'm home now."

"That would be great, hon, but you don't have to if you don't want to. I can make something or buy a sandwich. I know you don't like housewife-type duties." Sean smiled and kissed the top of her head. He took the last swallow of tea and walked to the front door, giving her a wink as he walked out.

Jill sat there a minute longer and then shook her head, trying to clear all the negative thoughts out.

On the drive back to work, Sean knew he had to continue his investigation of the Charmeins. He didn't want to share a lot of his suspicions about the odd couple with Jill until he had more information on them. As usual, he was trying to protect her.

♟ ♟

As Jill had suggested, the next morning she had Sean's lunch waiting for him. She left a note that she was going to the Charmeins and then heading into town. She had to buy some paint so Sean figured that meant she was going to Lebron, which had a few larger stores. She usually waited until she needed several tubes of paint and then bought online but he figured she was determined to complete the few paintings she needed before she went to New York and would purchase the colors she needed even though the prices were going to be higher. He decided to take this opportunity to go into work early but visit the town hall in Lebron first. He was positive he wouldn't run into Jill if she had also gone into Lebron since she would be going downtown to the art store. Although he loved the rural environment, he was sometimes frustrated with the too-slow pace of the life they lived. It was perfect for people who were retired but since he and Jill were climbing their own ladders to success sometimes it would be more convenient to have a mall or a major city within reasonable driving distance. Even though he and Jill could purchase what they needed online, they did occasionally need an item right away. Of course, with no internet at the cottage, they still had to drive into town to order something online. He could order from his store, but he preferred not to, only using his computer at work for work-related purchases.

Sean found Lebron's town hall and asked the clerk for a map that showed property boundaries. They had the same problem as Webster - the property didn't appear on their maps. It was like the property didn't exist. He thought about asking the clerk a few more questions, but she now had three people waiting in line for her attention and he needed to get to the bookstore. He wanted to stop at Lebron's library on his way back to the bookstore to look at the town's history and to see if the Charmein mansion was located in Lebron or if he could find any information about the property at all. He felt like he was wasting his time but he also knew he could eliminate the town hall and local libraries in his search if he came up blank. He thought he might have to go to the county's registrar of deeds next. They would surely have information about both Lebron's and Webster's properties.

Although Lebron's library was a bit larger than Webster's and the staff, like Webster's, was most helpful, he still did not find out anything about the mansion. Perhaps it wasn't in their family name, perhaps it was under another name and that's why neither town had any information under Charmein. As far as the towns were concerned, they didn't exist. So, before Sean went to the registrar of deeds, he decided he needed to do a little more nosing around the property to see if he could find some kind of plaque, maybe long buried, or something on the outside walls of the mansion that had an engraved name. Sean drove to his bookstore satisfied with this new direction he was going in.

♟ ♙

As time usually does, it passed quickly and Jill's trip to New York was upon them. Sean was still worried about her going to the city alone, but relieved that she would only be spending a week there. He knew she had to go, and he knew he had to support her.

Her bags sat at the front door. He had a cup of coffee for her as he sipped his own cup. She came into the room from her studio and he handed her the cup. She took one sip and handed it back.

"Thanks babe but I really don't have time for this. The taxi will be here in just a few minutes and I have to double-check everything I need to bring."

"Don't you mean 'triple-check'? I'm sure you've already gone through everything twice." Jill was an efficient packer and brought just the few articles of clothing she would need to meet with the gallery owners plus a pair of jeans and toiletries all condensed into one bag. Her portfolio case, of course, was the most important item to her and would allow her to carry on without having to wait for luggage that might get lost.

She smiled and taking her mug back and placing it on the table, took Sean's mug, placed it next to hers, and then turned to give him a big hug, kissing his face all over.

"Thank you, thank you, thank you, for believing in me. I don't know what I would do without you, Sean. I'll make you proud, I promise."

"You already make me proud. You know you will always have my support." They kissed right at the moment the taxi arrived. Sean gave her several more kisses and carried her bag out for her. Jill carried her portfolio - he knew she wouldn't let it go. The taxi driver had opened the trunk and the back door for her to enter but Jill jumped in the back seat after Sean put her one travel bag in there. He then closed the back door and after Jill put the window down, gave her another kiss. The driver shut the trunk and walked to the driver's side of the taxi. Jill leaned out the window waving and throwing kisses to Sean as they drove away. Sean stood watching the taxi until it was out of his sight.

A sadness swept over him as he turned towards the cottage. Then he turned towards the mansion and thought about the people living there. How, he wondered, how do people get this rich? There should be more of a division of wealth, not a small percentage having vulgar wealth while the majority of people are just trying to scrape out a living, often doing something they love to do, but struggling to pay the rent. They should be rewarded. Jill should be rewarded. She puts her heart and soul into what she loves to do. But here these eccentrics sit in their big mansion, drinking to excess apparently, doing nothing all day. And more than likely, if they've always had this wealth, they've never done anything with their lives. They never had to do anything. The major reason people work is to have a place to live, food to eat, clothes to wear. The majority don't want to throw money away on gambling or drugs or something wasteful like that. They just want to survive this life in a mostly comfortable way.

Now that Sean was completely depressed, he walked back into the cottage. He finished his coffee and decided to go into work early. He didn't like the sound of so much quiet without Jill around.

Jill faithfully called Sean at least once during the day and then again at night. Her excitement was contagious and although Sean missed her more than he let her know, he hung up feeling hopeful about their future. He had the bookstore, but he also had his writing. He took advantage of being alone by filling his nights with uninterrupted writing. He wouldn't let himself think about what a successful trip would mean for Jill. But the thoughts intruded upon his novel writing anyway. Every time he shook them away, they would return. He knew what this trip to New York would mean and although he was supportive of everything Jill did, he couldn't help thinking selfishly of what it meant for him. Sure, her pursuing her dreams allowed him to pursue his: a completed novel. He knew that when a publisher picked up his book, he would be on the book tour circuit. Plus, of course, he'd sell it in his own store and have a book-signing event. He knew several other bookstore owners and was sure they'd have book-signing events for him. And then Jill would be going to New York more regularly to have openings and promoting her art. It was what they both wanted, always. They still had plenty of time if they wanted the house in the suburbs and children. They had talked only briefly about it and most likely would have just one child, but he knew one of them had to be financially successful before any of the white-picket-fence scenario could become a reality.

The week passed by quickly and the day Jill was due home from New York Sean prepared a special dinner with her favorite red wine, Gnarly Head an Old Vine Zinfandel, and a crock pot chicken cacciatore on angel hair pasta. He had a garlic bread ready to warm in the oven. He bought her a bouquet of Freesia, her favorite flowers that were hard to find but after asking at the local florist in Webster he drove to Lebron and found a florist that specialized in more unique flowers. Jill had called from the airport and arrived minutes after Sean had shaved, showered, and dressed comfortably but neatly in Jill's favorite turquoise blue river driver shirt and jeans. He ran out the door to greet her as the taxi driver, the same man who'd picked her up, was taking her bag from the trunk. She came out of the back seat carrying her portfolio case and smiled as Sean took the case from her hand and kissed her.

"I have to pay the man, Sean. Do you have any money?"

"Oh sure, yes, one second, let me get my wallet." He ran back into the house and finding his wallet, ran back out. Jill was standing on the porch with her travel case and portfolio. Sean realized she looked very tired.

"How much?"

"Thirty-five." The man stood by his driver's door with his hand out. Sean took out two twenties and handed them to the man. The man nodded, got in the taxi, and drove off.

He ran back up to Jill who had walked into the cottage with her portfolio. He grabbed her travel case and followed her in.

"Are you hungry? I made you a wonderful meal. I can't tell you how happy I am to have you home." She was sitting on the couch, still holding her portfolio case. He took the case from her hands and she reluctantly let go. Then he put a glass of wine in her hand, unbuttoning her coat while kissing her neck and her face and touching her face.

"I just missed you so much, Jill, I can't tell you." Jill seemed to snap out of whatever stupor she was in and smiled at Sean, looking at him for the first time since she got out of the taxi. She didn't seem to be herself, though, and he wondered what was going on. He had talked to her from the airport and she sounded fine. Now, she seemed almost drugged.

"What's wrong? You sounded fine when I talked to you at the airport."

"I'm just tired, I was napping on the ride home. I guess coming back here to this cottage just hit me. This past week was so exciting and I guess I got caught up in all of it, you know. City life is so different from this rural living. There are parties and gallery openings and amazing restaurants, such a fast pace. You remember, the life we used to have. I guess I missed it a little and now, I'm back here where we are slaves to these people who live in a mansion while we squabble about spending too much money on a bottle of wine."

"But I thought we both wanted this, to get away from that life. The fast pace was killing us both, those were your words."

"I know, but can't I also miss it a little? It was exciting, too. It wasn't all negative."

Sean felt like her homecoming was not turning out the way he had planned. He was hoping for a nice dinner, conversation, and then love-making all night. He couldn't wait to hold her in his arms feeling her naked body wrapped in his.

"Look we'll do whatever you want, you know that, but can we just have a nice night together. I made chicken cacciatore with pasta and I, I just missed you so much, Jill."

Jill looked at him and saw the disappointment on his face. She knew he would do anything for her and stopped thinking about what they didn't have and focused on how lucky she was to have Sean. She pulled him close to her and kissed him.

"Dessert before supper?" Jill whispered in his ear. Sean picked her up and carried her to the bedroom.

The dinner was perfect, the wine the best complement, and the conversation exciting as Jill shared the positive feedback she got from all the gallery owners she'd met with.

"So how many gallery owners did you actually get to meet with?"

"Well, I had the appointments with Gallery NYC and The Joshua Gallery. But then I went to another artist's opening that I was invited to and met with the owner of 5th Avenue Gallery who took a quick look at my portfolio, which I didn't let out of my sight, and they are interested, too. His name was, oh, let me think, an unusual name, like Pieter or Pontriev."

"I hope you wrote all this down."

"Of course I did, and I have business cards from all of them, too. But everyone loved my work. Sean, it was so exciting. I can't believe how much positive feedback I got from everyone."

"So this was a good trip for you. It doesn't matter how much I rave about your work, you really needed to hear from someone else, someone with the credentials. And now you know. And other people know, too, how awesome you are." He leaned across the table and kissed her.

"You're right, it does help to hear from an objective outsider. After all, they aren't trying to get into my pants." Her sexy smile always knocked him out.

"Are you trying to seduce me, again?" The meal seemed to revive her and Sean knew things would soon be back to normal. Jill giggled and they left the dirty dishes right where they were.

Chapter 6

Your presence is requested at the home of
Noah and Charlotte Charmein.
The occasion: Dinner and drinks
Date: Sunday, October 20
Time: 6:30pm
Dinner will be served promptly at 7pm
after drinks and hors d'oeuvres in the parlor.
Dessert and coffee will follow dinner
after a short rest in the parlor.
We request that you arrive on time.

"So, do you think they'll be sending these invitations every month? You know, it's an exact duplicate with only the date changed. They must have someone print these up for them because they don't seem to know anything about computers. I can't imagine they printed these themselves. It was computer-generated, wasn't it?"

Jill inspected the invitation closely. The envelope was addressed to them and had been sent through the mail, another oddity since they lived just several hundred feet away. They must have had the gardener drop it in the mail. And then Jill thought 'or the housekeeper' but then she realized she was the housekeeper. Not officially but she hadn't seen the housekeeper around - maybe when they go to dinner at the Charmeins they will find out if she is still working there. For now, she is the 'gofer' for lack of a better title.

"Yeah, you know, it looks like it was hand-written. Like italic calligraphy. I played around with that when I was in college. It was fun. When girls in my dorm found out, they came to me to make up all the fancy announcements or any special posters we needed for things like, you know, fund raisers, things like that."

"You are just full of so many talents and I keep discovering more and more."

Jill smiled, nodding her head in agreement, and then taking a last gulp of her morning coffee, headed for the front door.

"Mustn't keep our landlords waiting! Time to do some errands - maybe I'll find out what we're having for dinner on Sunday. And if they'll actually have a dessert this time."

"Aren't you going to look through the rest of the mail? I waited for you; I knew you'd want to be the one to open the special invitation. I didn't really see anything else of interest in your mail, though."

"No, just junk mostly. I gave it a quick look. That can wait until later. I have to send some thank-yous to the galleries I met with in New York. I want them to keep me on their radar so they don't forget about me. Depending on what kinds of errands I have to do, I might just wait and do them later so I can mail the thank-yous at the same time. Are you going in early today?"

"Yes, this is my early day. Brenda and Jennie are on tonight. And since it is Saturday, they'll be there until 9. It's usually busy on Saturdays."

"Ok, then I'll see you back here at around 6?"

"Yup, have a great day, babe." Sean kissed Jill as she was running out the door and, finishing his coffee, gathered his briefcase and left right behind her.

♟ ♟

Sean and Jill arrived promptly at the Charmeins at 6:30pm, per their request. And again, Noah opened the door to greet them just seconds after Sean knocked. He couldn't resist using the large iron knocker on the front door. Something about the lion's head brought him back to the olden days with the enormous oak doors and elaborate door knockers, just like the one on the Charmeins' mansion. Noah gave him a disapproving look, as if Sean was behaving like a five-year-old and needed to be reprimanded for playing with the door knocker. But Noah didn't say anything and Sean could feel his face warming up. He and Jill entered and followed Noah, who was holding his drink, champagne of course, into the parlor. This time they'd brought a bottle of champagne since Charley had seemed disappointed with the wine they'd brought last time. Jill smiled as she handed the bottle to Charley who was lounging on the red velvet sofa, champagne glass in hand.

"I remembered." Jill was proud of herself and expected at least a thank you.

"Oh." Charley glanced at the label and just as quickly handed the bottle to Noah. Jill shook her head and giving Sean a side glance, sat down across from Charley. Noah handed her a glass which she took and swiftly downed the champagne. Sean stared at her and sipped his own champagne. Jill put her glass out indicating she would like a refill.

"Perhaps you should pace yourself, my dear." Noah filled her glass half full this time. Sean could almost feel the heat coming off her and put his hand on her shoulder which she shook off. He knew enough to leave her alone and focused on the Charmeins. He was hoping to find out more about them tonight.

But again, Noah beat him to it and dominated the conversation by questioning Jill.

"So, you've been to New York? And how was it? Did you enjoy yourself?"

Jill gave Sean an accusatory look. He knew she was wondering how Noah knew she'd been to New York.

"New York was fine, just fine."

"What did you do there, my dear?" The Charmeins both sat, glasses in hand, waiting for Jill to fill them in on her recent trip.

"I visited a few... uh." She was trying her best to give short answers, waiting for Sean to jump in and ask the questions he supposedly had for Noah. But he sat, as the Charmeins did, with a plastic smile on his face, just like a Ken doll in a store window, waiting for Jill's answers.

"Galleries, yes," Charley jumped in, "I've always loved the New York galleries. They have so much wonderful art."

Finally, Sean came to his senses and jumped into the conversation.

"Really, which ones? Did you and Noah live there at some time in your lives? Or are you from the New York area?"

"Oh, no, darling, we visited one or two galleries on a trip we took, a long time ago."

Sean didn't want the moment to end and tried another way in.

"So, you've lived here, your entire lives, or was it a family home and you inherited it?" At that point Noah stood and taking Charley's glass and placing it on the table, reached down to take her hand.

"Oh dear, we do have to cut this short, time for dinner. Perhaps we can continue after dinner." Noah and Charley walked their snail's pace into the dining room. Although, it was more like a dining hall with seating for at least twenty-four people. Both chandeliers were on brightening the room as if it was daylight. Several Tiffany lamps graced the buffets and tables against the walls. Jill wondered if they were real Tiffanys or knock-offs. She guessed they were the real thing. Noah took his place at the head of the table and Charley sat to his right, same as before. Sean and Jill took the same seats as last time as well, to Noah's left. The dinner, once again, was in the middle of the table kept warm by the chafing dishes. Noah removed the covers revealing tonight's dinner included a roast beef, with several slices ready to take, surrounded by small red potatoes and a casserole of peas and carrots. Removing the cloth covering from a basket revealed warm snowflake dinner rolls.

"Oh my, everything looks wonderful." Sean felt his stomach growl and hoped no one had heard it.

"Well, I'm so happy you approve. Please help yourselves to everything." Noah put a roll on Charley's plate, and then passed the basket to Sean and they all filled their plates.

"We, of course, have red wine to go with the beef so help yourself to that. Charley and I will continue with our champagne." He filled Charley's glass again.

They ate in silence for several minutes, each lost in their own enjoyment of every bite that entered their mouths and found its way to their stomachs. Sean didn't know when he'd felt such satisfaction and gratitude for what he was eating.

"Everything is done to perfection. I don't know how you do it. And, again, you cooked this yourselves?"

"Oh yes, we did. Just the two of us." Noah looked at Charley and they burst out laughing. Sean exchanged a look with Jill and they each put their forks down, feeling like they were both somehow the butt of a private joke between the Charmeins.

"Please continue eating. Don't be alarmed. We enjoy watching others eat what we have prepared. We get great satisfaction from it."

This sudden outburst was just the encouragement Jill needed to ask a question that she was more than mildly curious about.

"So, Charley, I was wondering, do you have cancer?" Sean, surprised by Jill's boldness, started coughing. He reached for his water and looked from Jill to Charley, waiting for her response. Charley put down her fork, picked up her champagne glass, and fixed a dead-pan stare on Jill.

"What makes you ask that, my dear?" A cold blast hit Jill like she'd just stepped out into a January Nor'easter. Not one to be put off so easily, Jill stared right back.

"Morphine is usually prescribed for someone who is in a lot of pain. I was just wondering if you had cancer since that often comes with a lot of pain." Sean started laughing, nervously, and moved Jill's wine glass away from her.

"Ok, my love, I think maybe we've had a little too much to drink. How about some more water?" And he filled her glass from the water pitcher on the table.

"I'm sure she meant no harm. Although I didn't expect asking her to do a few errands would give her the right to question the items on our shopping list. It really is none of your business. So, why don't we just leave it at that." Charley turned to Noah and without saying a word to him, he addressed Sean and Jill.

"Perhaps it is time you both finished your meal and we'll say our good-nights. I'm going to escort my wife to the bedroom and I expect you'll be gone when I return. Thank you for your company and I'll see you in the morning, Jill, when you come by for our list of errands we need you to take care of for us."

Sean stood as Noah helped Charley from the table. As they were turning to leave the room, Noah hesitated and, looking back at Sean, sprung yet another surprise on them.

"Oh yes, since we weren't expecting such a rude question to change the tone of the evening, we never had the opportunity to share our good news with you. Since Jill is no longer employed by the school, and we know the burden is now on you, Sean, to pay the bills, we are cutting your rent in half. For the time being. Perhaps next month we'll have a more pleasant visit. Good night." And, turning back to Charley, closed the dining room door behind them.

"What the hell was that?" Jill sat there, stunned, still staring at the dining room door.

"You got me. Crazy, that's what they are. But I think we'd better get out of here before Noah comes back. Who knows, he might come back with a shot gun." Sean took the last bite of roast beef on his plate and a sip from his wine glass.

At that comment, Jill jumped up and nearly ran to the dining room door, peeking out to make sure Noah wasn't standing there with a shot gun. She waved to Sean that the coast was clear and after he swallowed the last of his wine, he followed her to the front door.

Back at the cottage and feeling safe in their space, Sean made them each a mug of tea. Jill sat on the couch and reached for the mug when Sean brought it over.

"That has to be the most bizarre thing that has ever happened to us. I mean, 'a rude question', how was that a rude question? Did they imagine, even for a second, that it might be concern?" Jill was shaking her head, still upset by the impertinence of their landlords.

"I don't know, babe, there was a certain attitude in the way you asked it, kind of accusatory, you know?"

Jill set her mug down and turned to face Sean who had sat down on the couch beside her.

"What? Are you kidding? That was a legitimate question. If they don't want me to know what is going on in their lives, then maybe they should use someone else to do their errands."

"Babe, did you hear what Noah said before he left the room? He said they are cutting our rent in half. In half! That's pretty generous, I think. The least we can do is let them have their privacy."

Jill continued staring at Sean and then got up from the couch, grabbed her mug of tea spilling a little on the coffee table and went to her studio, slamming the door behind her.

Sean knew he had to let her cool off and hoped she would rethink the situation. He especially wanted her to think about the generous gift the Charmeins had given them by cutting their rent in half. They only had the one salary now and until Jill could get her art into a few of the New York galleries and actually sell some of it, they were going to have to live more frugally. Unless she got another part time or temporary job and he was pretty sure she didn't want to do that. But as the only bread-winner in the family now, he knew they really needed to cut back on their expenses. He finished his tea and after taking some notes on his novel, he went to bed.

Chapter 7

The next morning Jill was up and out of the house before Sean got up. He showered, dressed, and left for the bookstore. He was distracted all day, thinking about Jill, hoping she would agree with what he'd said last night but knowing he couldn't depend on that happening. He knew if he brought it up again things could get a lot worse and he wanted to avoid that. He had to somehow let her know he was on her side.

Several days passed. He was busy with the store - they had inventory and a couple of special events with book-signings and entertaining authors. It was a good week for him and he wanted to celebrate with an inexpensive, but still good, bottle of wine. He came home just three days after the blow up between he and Jill and found her sitting on the sofa, crying. He was sure she was feeling as stressed about their fight as he was and he went to comfort her but was surprised when she pulled back.

"What, Jill, what's wrong? Are you still upset about our fight? I want you to know I'm sorry, I agree with you that the Charmeins are an odd couple, but that's no reason for us to fight. We have to stick together, babe. I miss you, I missed you this week. Please, can we make up?"

"What are you talking about? You think I'm crying about our fight? That was days ago, Sean. No, this is not about that. This is far more important than our stupid fight. This is about trust and love and deceit and, and, just, just so much more than anything you can imagine." And she cried louder, getting up and pacing the room, unable to control her crying now.

"Please, tell me what is going on. Please." Sean couldn't imagine what this was about but he got the feeling the Charmeins had something to do with it.

Jill tried to compose herself for long enough to explain why she was so upset.

"I called the galleries, the two that I went to see, who were so interested in me and my work. Well, suddenly they aren't at all interested. It's like I have some contagious disease and they want nothing to do with me. They wouldn't even talk to me. They had their assistants tell me, 'Oh, we're very sorry Ms. Porter but we decided your work won't fit in our gallery after all. But thank you for contacting us and best of luck.' I didn't get to say a single word and then she just hung up! It was like she was reading from a script. And the weird thing was, they both said exactly the same thing. I just can't believe it."

"Wasn't there another gallery who was interested? Did you call them? I don't know babe, gallery owners are an odd bunch, I mean, they live in New York city and like you said, there are parties all the time and I'm sure lots of drugs. Who knows what is going on with them. They probably had some other artist who has money coming in and they bought a spot on their wall where they were going to hang your artwork. They seem like a pretty fickle bunch. And maybe this artist lives close by so they could bug the gallery daily." Sean was hoping he was showing his support but he knew he was just rambling. It didn't seem to help, either, and Jill cried louder.

"Babe, what can I do? Do you want me to call them and see if I can find out what is going on? I know, I'll pretend like I'm calling about your work and say I was interested in buying a piece and when were you going to be there. How does that sound? See if I can get any more information from them." Sean really did think this was a good idea and hoped Jill would too. She stopped crying for a minute and looked at Sean, nodding her head as she considered what he had said.

"That is a good idea. Maybe they'll tell you something more."

He was thrilled that he could actually help her. It seemed odd that they would drop her so quickly when they had set up appointments to meet with her and genuinely seemed interested in her work. He dialed the number and asked to speak to the owner whose name was on the business card.

"May I ask who is calling, please?" The assistant was very professional. They certainly didn't sound like a gallery that partied and got stoned all the time. He quickly made up a name choosing one of the characters in his novel, giving himself a slight accent.

"Yes, of course, this is Mr. Grant Thornfield of Thornfield Industries."

"One moment." And he was put on hold. He smiled at Jill and she actually smiled back at him.

"Hello, this is Daphne Williams, how may I help you?"

"Yes, hello Ms. Williams, this is Mr. Grant Thornfield of Thornfield Industries. I heard you had a new artist coming to your gallery and wanted to know when I might see some of her work. The artist is Jill Porter."

"Oh, well, I'm so sorry Mr. Thornfield, but we decided her work won't fit in our gallery after all. But thank you for contacting us."

"Oh, that is really too bad. Do you know of any other galleries that might carry her work? I really would love to own a piece."

"No, I'm sorry I don't. But best of luck." She hung up without another word and Sean sat there looking at the phone, surprised at her abruptness.

"Well, what did they say?" Jill sat next to him, her eyes looking bloodshot and her nose red from wiping.

"Almost what you told me the assistant told you, verbatim. Isn't that odd?"

"What is going on? This is crazy, Sean. Just crazy. And you know the craziest part about all of this? Somehow, I don't know how, but I think the Charmeins are involved in this."

"Babe, how is that possible? They don't know which galleries you went to, and there are so many in New York city so how could they be involved?"

"How exactly, Sean. Obviously, you somehow must have let it drop which galleries I was visiting. That was the very first question Noah asked me, about going to New York. How did he know this? You must have told him. I wasn't here all week, remember? And suddenly he's asking me about my trip to New York. What does it sound like to you? And Charley, she finished my sentence. I never said galleries, she did!"

Sean sat on the couch thinking about what Jill had just said. She didn't trust him. She thought he was conspiring with the landlords. How could she not trust him? How could she possibly believe that about him? He would never do anything to hurt her. He only wanted the best for her, always. He thought about Noah mentioning the New York trip to Jill. He was so careful not to say anything to them about his and Jill's life. How could Noah know this? He hadn't even talked to him while Jill was away. And he didn't know many people in town and he only told the two women who work for him that Jill was in New York, no one else. And she was right, too, Charley had said 'galleries'. Jill never said the word. It was as if they knew, as if they know, what is happening in their lives before they even tell them. And then a light bulb went off; it could only mean one thing. He jumped up off the couch and ran to get a pad of paper and pen.

"What are you doing? Where are you going, Sean?" He put his finger to his lips signaling her to not speak.

"What?" Jill was confused and waited for Sean to write on the paper one word: *Bugged.*

"What do you mean..." Sean frantically zipped his mouth to get her to stop talking and handed her the pad of paper.

She wrote, '*What is bugged? Our house?*'

Sean wrote in large letters, '*YES!*'

Jill sat back on the couch, shaking her head in disbelief. But she knew that this was the only thing that made sense if Sean was being honest with her. And she had no reason to doubt him.

They spent the rest of the night writing to each other, sure that they were onto something. They also looked around the house, removing light bulbs, looking under the bed and in other places they thought wires might have been set up with microphones to listen to their conversations. They decided that if they found any microphones they would not disturb them. They wanted to use this information, which they felt confident was correct, to their advantage. They could actually set up false conversations and then see if the Charmeins mentioned anything at their monthly dinners, which would prove that they were definitely listening in on every conversation Sean and Jill had.

Around midnight Sean realized he was getting tired and since he had an early day the next morning, he had to

get some sleep. He received one last written message from
Jill:

*"What do we do about having sex? They must be listening
to that, also."*

Sean hadn't thought of this and just shook his
head and leaning toward Jill, kissed her good night.

"We'll figure it out. I can't think anymore tonight."
He whispered as quietly as he could.

The next morning Sean got up to the smell of
coffee. He took his shower, got dressed, and found not
only coffee ready for him but also a grilled cheese with
tomato sandwich and a brown bag lunch sitting on the
kitchen table. Jill turned to him when he entered the room.
She was sitting at the table eating her own grilled cheese
and tomato sandwich with her coffee.

"Good morning - thanks for the breakfast, this is
great, and my sandwich." Jill opened her eyes wide and put
a finger to her mouth. Sean sat down and wrote on the
pad of paper they used for their shopping list:

*"We need to appear normal - the last thing I want is for
them to be suspicious that we are on to them."*

Jill nodded, smiled, and gave him a thumbs up.

After breakfast Sean headed off to work and Jill
went to the Charmeins to get the errand list. She was sure
Noah would be ruder and more abrupt with her than
usual. She was surprised instead when, after opening the
door before she had barely knocked, he greeted her with a
smile and invited her in.

"Good morning, my dear, won't you come in?"

Jill hesitated wondering if he had an axe behind his
back. She didn't have the least bit of trust in him or
Charley and he seemed to sense that. He chuckled and

taking her arm and giving her more of a tug than she expected, pulled her into the house.

"I thought we should show you exactly what we expect of you now that you will be taking care of the upkeep of our home. It really has all worked out perfectly since we just let our housekeeper go last week. Although I'm sure you are quite devastated by the news from the galleries you visited in New York, I'm sure it is all for the best. After all, Sean really doesn't want to let you out of his sight. He cares very deeply for you, but I'm sure you already know that. Anyway, follow me."

Jill stood at the front door, unable to move, everything Noah had just said to her was running around and around in her head. 'I'm their housekeeper now? They knew about the galleries, which confirms they are listening to our conversations, and it's all for the best? But there's even more, the something about Sean not wanting me out of his sight?'

Noah, who had been rattling off the various duties that he expected her to do around the house, realized she wasn't following him and turned to her.

"Come along now, I haven't got all day." His tone changed to one of impatience. She obediently ran up to him, fearful now of the man who minutes before was talking to her like she was a bit of an imbecile with skills not much beyond vacuuming, mopping floors, and cleaning toilets. She followed him in a daze; not only stunned by this turn of events but also by the opulence and obvious extravagance of the furnishings in the great house. She had never seen such wealth; except maybe in Architectural Digest. She thought of places like the mansions in Newport, Rhode Island. The great wealth of the Vanderbilts was known around the world. She remembered the conversation she and Sean had before the first time they'd visited the Charmeins. Little did she realize how close to the truth they might be.

Noah led her from room to room. There had to be more than twenty in the house, many with their own bathrooms. As they walked from room to room, Noah snapped orders for how each were to be cared for - of course, the majority of them were never used and so wouldn't need any cleaning except an occasional dusting and vacuuming.

"The few that are used will only need cleaning and the linens changed when we have company staying with us."

"I thought you didn't have any family."

"I didn't say family, I said company. Please pay attention." Noah moved quickly through the house, explaining what was required of her. She followed as if she were a tourist in a museum.

"You really should have brought a pad to take notes. Unless you have an eidetic memory." He chuckled at what he obviously thought was humorous.

"Oh, one very important thing you absolutely must remember: Do not EVER go into Charley's room. EVER. Do you understand? It is this room right here. She takes care of her own cleaning, or I help her with it, so you must never go in there. Please try to remember this." Jill stared at the great double doors and tried to imagine the size of the room and what it might look like. Noah obviously didn't understand that when you tell someone to never do something, that is all they can think about doing. She was determined that one day she would get a peek in this most secretive room.

He walked down the imperial staircase and back to the front door which he opened and as Jill walked out, handed her the list without a word, quickly closing the door behind her. She stood looking at the two great doors with the lion's head knocker for several minutes before walking back to the cottage.

Sean had a busy day and came home tired, hoping to relax and unwind with a glass of wine. He hoped everything worked out when Jill went to get the errand list from Noah; he just wasn't up to any more drama caused by his landlords. Jill usually called him at work during the day but since he never heard from her, he hoped that was a good sign.

He walked in the house and Jill was walking towards him, slipping a jacket on as she quickly pushed Sean out the door.

"What are you doing? What's going on, babe?"

"Car, coffee shop, now."

The last thing Sean wanted to do was drive somewhere but Jill jumped into the driver's side so he got in on the passenger's side.

"What's up? Did you have a confrontation with Noah?"

"Can we just wait until we go to the coffee shop to talk. I want to get as far away from here as we can before we discuss them. You just won't believe it, Sean."

Sean took the opportunity to close his eyes and rest on the drive into town. He dozed off for a few minutes and before he knew it, he was jolted awake when the car came to a stop in front of the Webster Café. As they walked towards the front door, a man wearing a dirty red parka, with hair that looked like it hadn't been washed in a month, pants too long with the cuffs rolled up and boots that looked at least a size too big was hanging out in front of the Café. He seemed to be pacing, like he was waiting for someone to show up. They both eyed him suspiciously and Sean expected him to hold out his hand for money but instead the man looked directly at them and folding his arms across his chest, quickly moved out of their way and down the alley next to the Café, looking back over his shoulder as if he thought they might follow him.

Sean looked at Jill and raising his eyebrows, looked at her and then towards the odd man.

"Must be their resident homeless person."

"I don't know, he was pretty sad looking. Do they even have a shelter for homeless people in this town?" Jill was always concerned about those less fortunate.

They found a booth inside and Sean ordered a Rolling Rock and Jill ordered a glass of Chardonnay.

"Will you be having dinner tonight?" The waitress, Dolly, who was also the owner, put their drinks on the table. She always had a smile for everyone who came into her place. It was hard to say no to someone so pleasant.

"I think we'll have something light tonight, Dolly." Jill looked at the menu and made her decision quickly.

"I'll have a Caesar's Salad. Dressing on the side."

Sean took another minute and then decided on the cheeseburger with mashed potatoes instead of fries.

"That's something light?" Jill laughed.

"Well, I could have gotten the fries. Mashed potatoes seem lighter, don't they?" Dolly shook her head 'no' and laughed. She took the menus and started to walk away but Jill had a question.

"Dolly, when we came in there was a man out front, dirty red parka, looked pretty sad. I was wondering, is there a homeless shelter around or someplace he could go to sleep?"

"Oh, you must be talking about Stirling. Yeah, he is a pretty sad case, at least what I know about him."

She'd piqued Jill's interest - Sean knew she had to know more.

"Really? What do you know about him?"

"Well, his parents were killed when he was a boy, seven or so, and he was in and out of foster homes and different institutions. I guess there was no family or no one wanted him. There was a lot of abuse though, not good. The boy just didn't develop, you know, in the head. Didn't have proper schooling. He has a little shack he lives in and the townspeople mostly take care of him, make sure he has blankets and heat in the winter. I feed him regularly but he gets food from other folks, too. We take care of him best we can. Sometimes you'll find him sleeping on a bench in the park down the street. He stays right around here, just kind of wanders all day. Like I said, not right in the head. That's about all I know."

"And his name is Stirling? Is that a last name?"

"Don't know, that's all anyone knows him by. Let me get your meal on before you starve to death."

"Wow, that's quite a story. Maybe something you can use in a novel, Sean. I mean, the poor guy, especially if no one wanted him. So, you lose your parents and then you are sent away and you are put into abusive situations. How awful is that? I wish we could help him, maybe give him some food."

Sean didn't have quite the same-sized heart that Jill had and knew he needed to focus on paying their own bills and feeding him and Jill. He couldn't think about the one homeless guy in town who was taken care of by all the townspeople. He wanted to get back to whatever it was Jill had to share with him and the reason they couldn't talk at home. Wasn't that why they were at the Webster Café in the first place?

"So, you had something you wanted to talk to me about, remember?" Jill suddenly perked up and lowering her voice, looked around the Café. There were a couple of people at the counter and only two other couples several booths away from them.

"You just won't believe Noah. Oh my God, Sean, you won't believe what happened today. First, he took me on a tour of the house."

"That's interesting - you must have enjoyed that. Is it as opulent as we thought it was?"

"Yes, of course, but that isn't the point. It wasn't a tour and he thought I would enjoy seeing the place, it was more like, 'and this is what we need you to clean since you are now our cleaning lady.' Isn't he incredible?"

"What? How did you go from doing errands for them to cleaning that huge, friggin' mansion?"

"I have no idea. I was in shock, and you wouldn't believe how rude he was, as if I already was the hired help. But the place is amazing. I felt like I was walking through one of the Vanderbilt mansions in Newport."

"Well, that doesn't surprise me." Dolly came back to the table and put the Caesar Salad in front of Jill and the burger in front of Sean.

"Can I get you kids anything else? More drinks?" Dolly stood over them with her hands on her hips, big smile on her face.

"No, I think we're good. Thank you, Dolly."

"Ok. I'll be back when it's time for dessert. Have a fresh pumpkin pie today." And she left the two to enjoy their meals.

"Anyway, back to the Charmeins. What did you say when you realized you were expected to clean the place now?" Sean took a big bite of his cheeseburger - Jill had to admit it looked really good but she was glad she got the salad. Her stomach was too upset to eat anything heavy.

"I didn't say anything, Sean. I told you, I was in shock. I was trying to figure out why he was taking me through the rooms and I was thinking it was a tour more than anything else but somewhere in the back of my mind I realized he was giving me instructions about cleaning each room. Oh yeah, get this. Each room, except Charley's room. I was instructed to NEVER, EVER go into Charley's room. How odd is that!"

"Really. That is odd. Never, ever, he said those words exactly?"

"Yes, exactly like that. Oh, and one more thing. When he was taking me from room to room, he said most of them wouldn't need much cleaning just a dusting from time to time. But when they had guests, those are the rooms that would need cleaning."

"Guests? They have guests? I thought they didn't have any family?"

"Yeah, exactly what I said, and Noah corrected me and said, I didn't say family, I said, guests, or no, company, he said company. Implying that they do have guests who aren't family but friends, I guess."

They ate in silence for a few minutes, each lost in their own thoughts.

"So, what do you think? What should I do, Sean. I mean, I wasn't expecting to make this my full-time job. And oh yes, the most important part, we're right, they are listening to us. He told me how devastated I must be that the galleries I visited in New York didn't work out. So obviously they were listening to us talk about it. Oh my God, Sean, this is crazy. We can't live like this. We need to move."

"Yeah, this is getting really creepy. Ok, we'll start looking around. I'm sure they feel justified in putting you to work for them since they just cut our rent in half. But we have no privacy anymore. And unless we decide to tear the place apart, we may never find the bugs that they set up in the cottage."

"Oh yeah, I forgot about that, about the rent cut. Well, we'll have to find a place that is close to where your store is, that will save on gas. And maybe I can find something there, too. The most important thing is that we still have time to work on what is important to us, my painting and your novel. We need another salary. And we have no idea what the rents are closer to town. I do remember looking around Webster and there really wasn't anything available - not many apartments. I seem to remember that Lebron is the same, not many apartments available."

"Maybe we can look for a house." Sean didn't really think about the costs, he was just throwing out options.

"Sean, we have no down payment, I don't think we can do that. Although it would be great to have our own home." Jill looked wistfully into her glass of wine and downed the last swallow.

"Or, maybe a new home is closer than we think." He waited for her to think about what he was saying but after a few minutes as Jill continued staring into her empty wine glass, he knew he was alone in his thinking.

"Babe, did you hear me?"

"What, no I was lost. I'm sorry, what did you say?"

"I said, maybe a home is closer than we think."

"A home, no, I don't know what you're talking about. What home?"

"Well, more like… a mansion." His eyes were looking down and he briefly looked up to catch her expression. It was priceless; a puzzled, questioning look covered her face.

"What are you saying, Sean? I hope you aren't saying what I think you're saying." Right at that moment Dolly came over.

"How about that pumpkin pie? I have at least two slices left. Coffee, tea, or another Chardonnay and Rolling Rock?" They looked up and if Dolly could read facial expressions, she would have seen guilt all over their faces. Jill spoke up.

"One piece, two forks, one tea, cream, one coffee, black."

"Alrighty, coming right up!" Dolly picked up their dirty dishes and walked away with a smile as wide as her face.

"Sean? I'm waiting. Please explain." Jill's face went back to the same puzzled, questioning look. But now he detected anxiety, also, and maybe a little fear.

"Ok, look, they have no family. They are both up there in age. It isn't like they are nice people or anything. If they were regularly giving to the poor and the needy, I wouldn't even think of something like this. But they are awful people. Assholes, really. You have to agree with me there."

"Yes, I do, but it sounds like you have something more sinister in mind than calling them names."

Sean couldn't suppress a laugh.

"I'm not trying to be funny."

"I know. I'm not really laughing at that. I guess I'm laughing at the whole story that has become our lives now. And we can add another crazy chapter to it."

"Yeah, but this 'chapter' in our lives could land us in jail. Have you thought that far ahead?"

"That will never happen." Sean noticed Dolly heading their way and shifted in his seat.

"Ok, one piece of delicious pumpkin pie, two forks, a tea with cream, sugar's on the table there, and a coffee, black. Are we all set for now?"

"Yes, perfect, thanks." Dolly went back to the counter to take care of one of the couples that was paying their check.

"So, what makes you so sure that will never happen?"

"Because no one seems to know anything about them. I've gone to the town hall in Webster and in Lebron and no one knows anything about the mansion or the people living in it. It is as if they don't even exist."

"But Sean, he told me they have company, which could be friends. Ok, so no family, but there could be other people they know, even from out of the country. How would we know? We really don't know anything about them. They've been very secretive even though they know so much about us, by now."

"I think he's bluffing. He probably suspects that we would try something so he just said they have company stay there sometimes. At this point I wouldn't trust or believe anything they say."

Jill was quiet for a minute, stirring sugar in her tea. Sean took a bite of the pie that had a dollop of real whipped cream on top.

"This really is good - real whipped cream, too. You should try it." Jill dipped her pinky in the whipped cream and licked it off. She was deep in thought, Sean could almost hear the wheels turning in her head.

"So, what do you propose we do?"

"Something painless for both of us."

"Poison?" Sean nodded.

"I guess there really is no other way. I wouldn't want to deal with anything else, too gruesome. No blood." She whispered the last word and looked around. Dolly was tallying up her sales for the day. Jill looked around the Café and noticed they were the only ones there now. She looked at the clock on the wall above the front door and saw the time.

"Jesus, Sean, it is 9:15. I'm pretty sure they close at 9. Dolly is closing up the register. We should pay and go." She took a couple of bites of the pie and called over to Dolly.

"Sorry Dolly, we'll pay if you want to close up."

"Take your time, I still have a few things to do but I would appreciate payment now. But no need to rush with your drinks and pie."

Sean took out his wallet and went to the counter. Dolly gave him the check and he paid with cash. Jill took another bite of the pie and sipped her tea.

"It is good pie, we should have gotten two pieces." She smiled at Sean.

"You can have the rest, babe."

"No, I'm done. I'm just going to drink my tea. But thanks."

Sean ate the last of the pie and drank his coffee. They were both quiet for a while. They seemed to have run out of words to say. Jill finished her tea and sat back in the booth, signaling that she was ready to leave. Sean drank the last of his coffee and they both got up to leave.

"Thanks, folks. You have a nice night now."

"Thanks, Dolly." Sean opened the door and they left.

Chapter 8

The coffee Sean had was kicking in, so he drove them home. They were too exhausted from the evening's conversation and the ride home was quiet. Sean caught Jill dozing off, but then she'd sit up a little straighter. He knew she liked to keep him company but knew she was also afraid he might doze off, so she considered herself his backup eyes. They got ready for bed as quietly as possible and both fell asleep just minutes after slipping under the covers.

The morning was similarly quiet. They were both so aware now of the house being bugged that they knew they couldn't talk about anything to do with the Charmeins. But they also knew they had to engage in some conversation so the Charmeins wouldn't know they were onto them. They wanted everything in the house to appear normal.

"So, I'll be home around my usual 6pm, ok? Have a great day, babe. Are you going to paint?"

"Yeah, I might. I do have 'the errands' and I don't know what else, yet." Sean knew that was specifically for the Charmeins.

Sean kissed her good-bye and then took the lunch she'd made for him.

"Thanks for the lunch." Jill gave him a big hug and whispered in his ear.

"I wrote a note."

"Ok, see you tonight." And he left. He drove out of the driveway and once away from the house, pulled over and took the note out of the lunch bag.

'I'm in, whatever you want to do.' It was signed with a heart. Now he had a mission.

Jill finished her coffee and cereal and after putting on her rattiest pair of jeans and a sweatshirt with sneakers, she walked up to the Charmeins. She had no idea if she was supposed to bring her own cleaning supplies and assumed they would have them for her.

Once again, she barely touched the door and it was flung open by Noah.

"Well, good morning my dear. And how are you this fine morning? Ready to go to work. Great! Let me show you where the cleaning supplies are. I hope you remember everything I told you yesterday."

Jill wasn't even sure if she was going to be cleaning today but she was glad she decided to wear her painting clothes. She followed Noah to the kitchen where he showed her the cleaning supplies.

"Now, the kitchen needs the floor mopped. The dirty dishes are placed in the dishwasher; you may have to wash a few pots. But, mostly just the floor. See, we're making your job easy. And when you are finished, I'll have the errand list for you."

Jill looked around the kitchen and decided this would be the last chore. An industrial-sized space there was everything any great cook could want in a fully-stocked kitchen. Stainless everywhere, with a huge refrigerator and freezer next to it. The stove with six burners and a warming area and a flat griddle made her drool with envy. She would enjoy cooking so much more if she had a setup like this.

She took out the dust cloth and furniture polish and headed off to the upstairs bedrooms. She figured there would be the least amount of work to do there. And she was right. There was very little to do in most of them. She did take her time admiring the many antiques that sat dust-free on the nightstands and tables around the bedrooms and in various locations around the house. The one thing she did notice was that there were no family portraits. Anywhere. She thought she would at least find a portrait of Charley over the fireplace in the parlor but she found instead an enormous painting of a landscape which she guessed was in Italy. She tried to see the signature but several of them were up too high to read. This was a special treat for her and she was excited to look at all the artwork throughout the house, many by artists she was quite familiar with, like Modigliani and Boccioni. She loved Boccioni's use of color and could look at them all day but she really needed to finish the dusting and get on with her chores.

She checked the rooms and with most of them she gave the finger test. If no dust came up, she skipped them. She checked the bathrooms and did the same thing - if it was obvious that it had not been used, she would give the sink and top of the toilet tank a quick wipe and leave the room as it was.

There were two rooms that appeared to have been used. This surprised her. One of the beds had been slept in and she took the sheets off and threw them into the laundry chute. She did at least remember those instructions when Noah had given her the tour. She wondered if this was Noah's room or if he slept in different rooms so that she and Sean would think the Charmeins had company. That sounded more plausible to her. In the other room, the bed looked like someone took a nap on the bed but never went under the sheets. She checked the blanket and sheets and everything looked in order so she just straightened the blanket on top and rearranged the pillows. She took a little more care dusting these two rooms and cleaning their bathroom's toilets and sinks, even though there was no sign of having been used. She remembered that Noah did say 'Charley's room', not 'our room'. And, with so many bedrooms in the house, she figured all the other rooms could very possibly be Noah's rooms. He most likely slept in a different room every night. Of course, he wasn't the one making the beds or cleaning the bathrooms so it didn't matter to him which room he slept in. If this was her house and she had all these rooms to choose from, she would probably sleep in different rooms from time to time as well, as long as she wasn't doing the cleaning. And when people live in mansions, you could probably assume that they weren't doing the cleaning. She thought of people like Bill Gates and Oprah. No doubt they had so much time to do everything they wanted to do with their lives because they had people doing their laundry, cleaning their homes, making their meals.

For years that was called 'the wife.' But with two income couples, that had mostly changed. Although she did remember working as a cocktail waitress while in college, one of the other waitresses who, working the 7pm - 2am shift after her kids had been fed and their homework done, had a husband who worked days and he considered himself the only one who worked and never helped with any of the housecleaning or cooking. Jill told this woman her husband was a dick but hey, we each have to decide for ourselves what is considered abuse. The sad thing is, a lot of women don't realize when they are being abused by their husbands. Generation after generation of women just accepted this abuse, unable to escape the pattern that they grew up seeing at the hands of their own fathers. Thoughts like these always brought her back to

Sean and how loving, supportive, and non-chauvinistic he was.

She finished up in the two rooms and was about to go back to the kitchen to return the dust cloths and furniture polish when she almost ran right into Noah.

"Don't forget to vacuum. You'll find the vacuum in the kitchen pantry. We do get dust kitties around. Charley is not very fond of those and has an eye for them so don't try to short-cut because she'll see them. And when you finish, I may not be available so here is the shopping list for today. Good day." And he turned towards Charley's room. He looked back over his shoulder with his hand on the doorknob.

"Oh, one more thing. We had to let our gardener go as well, so do you think your husband could do some raking in the yard? We would like to have this done before the snows come. All the tools that he'll need are in the carriage house. The keys are on the hook next to the back kitchen door." Noah turned away and opening the door to Charley's room barely a crack, snuck in before Jill could answer. He obviously assumed that this new chore would be done. Now Noah was expecting Sean to work for them as well. If that was his plan, then he'd better not charge them anything for rent. She wanted to get the cleaning done so she could call Sean and let him know this latest bit of news.

After putting the cleaning products away, she looked for the vacuum. She hoped it wasn't something from the dark ages when vacuums weighed as much as a six-foot tall man. She looked in the kitchen pantry that held every kind of cleaning equipment imaginable and found a very modern Dyson which was not only cordless but also lightweight. She ran up the stairs and focusing on the two rooms that seemed to have been used, vacuumed areas that would have been walked on, taking care to look for any dust kitties in corners or along the baseboards. She checked each room for any sign of dirt or dust and when she was satisfied, she put the vacuum away. Her last chore was to mop the kitchen floor and when she was done, she left to do the errands. She'd spent far more time than she thought she would, but now that she knew the routine she was sure it wouldn't take her as long the next time. But she did plan on taking some time to view more of the artwork. That was a treat she hadn't expected and she wanted to study more closely the beautiful paintings. Of course, if they actually went through with Sean's plan, they would be hers to view whenever she wanted. She shivered, partly from the cold air as she walked back to the cottage but mostly because she hadn't thought about 'the plan' and now that she was, she was positive it was not the way to go. They would just have to find another apartment. Until then, she would do the cleaning, realizing that it was helping with their rent, and continue painting and looking for other galleries to sell her work. She was not going to give up hope.

♟ ♟

Sean decided to do some more research at the library instead of eating his lunch at his desk while working as usual. He could have used the internet at work, but he didn't want to leave any incriminating evidence on his computer about what he and Jill were planning. He even thought about going a few towns away but he was already driving to Lebron everyday which was more than 20 miles from where they lived. He was trying to keep their gas usage down - he was trying to keep all expenses down since they were living on his one salary now. He knew Jill could get another paying job but since their rent had been cut by half, he wanted to see how Jill was handling the added responsibilities. If she wasn't also painting, doing what she loved, he would know that this arrangement wasn't working. He hoped the Charmeins weren't wearing her out. But then, when he thought about this new plan, he had mixed emotions. He was afraid, definitely, but would never share those feelings with Jill. If she felt any hesitation on his part she would be out. He had to feel confident about the double murder they were planning. Double murder. He had never thought of it that way before but that is what it was. They would be killing Noah and Charley Charmein. He felt sick and put his sandwich back in the bag. The library was empty except for him and when he bent over to put his head down, he was grateful that he had decided to go to the library now instead of waiting until he got out of work at 6pm when he knew it would have been busier. At 2pm, it was quiet and mostly deserted. He really needed this time to himself.

Along with his feeling of nausea, suddenly overwhelmed by guilt and sadness that he could get to this place in his life, a lump formed in his throat causing him to cough. The librarian walked into the room with the reference books where the computers were set up for public use, and stopped to look at him, wondering if she needed to call for help or simply bring the man a glass of water. Sean held up his hand indicating he was ok. She smiled and went about reshelving the few books she carried in her arms. He shook his head, finished his sandwich, and continued with his research. To move forward he told himself this was research for a book he was working on. That made it ok. He knew he was only fooling himself, but he had to get through this. He thought, again, that it was a good idea to use a public computer because he didn't want the kind of information he was searching for to be somehow linked to him. Although he knew they could narrow it down to the time he was on this computer since he had to log in to use it. They might wonder why he didn't use his computer at work, which could make him look even more suspicious. They would know it was him, whoever 'they' were. Again, the sick-to-his-stomach feeling took hold of him.

Cyanide. That was the word that kept coming up. He briefly thought about iocaine powder - which was odorless, tasteless, and dissolves instantly in water, the most-deadly poison known to man - unfortunately it was fictional. Sounded perfect, though. The taste of cyanide is bitter, so they'd have to be sure they used it in a dessert so they could sweeten it. This was ideal because although the Charmeins always mentioned dessert in their monthly invitations, they had yet to serve any. So, that is it. He and Jill would bring dessert and put the cyanide in that. Of course, they would excuse themselves from having any, claiming the meal had stuffed them so they could leave the dessert for Noah and Charley.

Now he had to find out where and how to purchase some without raising any suspicion. Although, after reading about it on the Centers for Disease Control website, he learned it can be harvested from the pits of many fruits. So that was the answer. No one would be suspicious if they were buying apples or apricots at the supermarket. They would make a fruit tart or pie and use the seeds to poison the dessert. It was a perfect plan.

Sean finished his lunch and drove back to work. He put the plan completely out of his mind and focused on his work, filling orders and taking inventory.

♟ ♙

Once Jill had delivered the groceries to the Charmeins, she went back to the cottage to open a can of soup for lunch and look through the newspaper she had picked up to check out apartments in Lebron and also scan the help wanted section. Maybe she could find something waitressing; she had done it in college and although she didn't like it, she had done ok with tips. Lebron had several fancy restaurants so she should be able to pick up some good money there. She had hoped she was beyond this but she also knew waitressing was something she could fall back on if needed. She was not enjoying relying on one pay check.

She opened the paper to the job section first. She skimmed through them; slim pickings, as she expected, and most were for entry-level positions at fast food restaurants. She definitely was not stooping that low although she remembered back in college when she told a guy she'd met at a party that she was a Fine Arts major he joked, 'oh, you mean a can-I-take-your-order major' and then he laughed like an idiot. Except Sean. He was genuinely interested and asked what kind of art she painted. As she reminisced for several minutes one particular job jumped out at her. 'Webster Elementary School, Teacher Wanted, Art background a plus, starting salary commensurate with experience. Send resume to Ginny Poole, Principal, Webster Elementary.'

Jill sat up taller and re-read the entire ad. She couldn't believe it. That was the job she'd been let go from because supposedly another teacher had come back and they'd given it to her.

"What the fuck!" She dialed Sean and then remembered the bugs in the house. She slammed the phone down. Somehow, she just knew the Charmeins were involved. She didn't know how but she was sure it was them. It had to be. There was no reason for the school to have let her go. Someone had made them. But how could they have that much power when, according to Sean, he couldn't even find them in either Webster's or Lebron's town hall property records, neither one had any information on the Charmeins or the mansion they lived in. She tried to calm down. She thought this through; there could be another option. Maybe, just maybe, it didn't work out with the other teacher. Maybe they really were looking for a teacher again. Maybe she should resend her resume.

She felt more hopeful and finished her soup, scanning the 'For Rent' section for apartments in the Lebron area.

♟ ♟

When Sean came home, he was in a good mood and found Jill in her studio, painting. She hadn't painted since the galleries in New York cancelled. He knew she had a show coming up in Madison in about a week and although he was sure she had enough work for that show, seeing her in her happy place made him happy. He walked into the studio carrying two glasses of her favorite wine, Babcock Chardonnay. She turned and smiled taking the glass from his hand and, after clinking glasses, gave Sean a big kiss.

"It is nice to see you painting and in a good mood. Anything interesting happen today?"

"Yes, I was inspired by the paintings at the Charmeins - beautiful and by some of my favorite artists. And after I did the errands, I was looking at the paper and found that the job I had at the school, is available again. So, I'm resending my resume."

Sean's expression changed.

"What, are you kidding me?"

"No, sweetie, I thought the same thing and then I said, well, this teacher didn't work out and so she left and now the position is open again. So, I'm sending them my resume. Hopefully they'll want me back. I mean, they already know me so, I think it could be possible that they'd want me back, don't you? I know the kids liked me and I got along with the other teachers, too.

"Ok, I didn't see it that way but you're right. That is a possibility." They clinked glasses again and sat on the futon in Jill's studio.

"I don't want to interrupt you if you want to keep painting."

Jill got up off the futon and walked out of the room. Sean pointed up at the ceiling to indicate someone might be listening. Jill nodded and they walked out the front door and got into Sean's pickup.

"So, I looked for an apartment in Lebron - nothing available, I mean, not even a single apartment for rent. Maybe we should go to a realtor. Sometimes apartments don't even make the papers, you need to sign up with a realtor."

"Yeah, as long as it doesn't cost us. Sometimes the person looking has to pay. Anyway, I wanted to talk to you about something."

They sat facing each other in the front seat of his truck. Sean got really serious and Jill knew what it was about before he said a word. She started shaking and leaning forward, put her elbows on the dashboard.

"Sean before you say anything, I have to say something. We can't do this, I don't want to. We'll move, we'll find a place. We have to. I'm afraid something will go wrong and we'll get caught."

He grabbed her and held her, feeling her shaking all over.

"Babe, it's ok. Don't worry, you won't have to do a thing. I'll take care of everything." Jill pulled away from him, trying to find the loving Sean she knew in his dark brown eyes.

"Really, you want to go through with this? I was hoping we would be on the same page and that you would agree that doing it was a bad plan, too risky. I just can't, Sean."

Sean stared out the front window of the truck. He thought they had a plan and now everything was changing. He knew he had to go along with Jill or she just might leave him. He couldn't live with himself if that happened.

"Ok, we'll see if we can find an apartment. But if we can't then we'll have to rethink our original plan. Ok?"

Jill nodded agreement but he knew it wasn't sincere. He knew he would have to go solo on this plan. He thought it was a perfect plan and the more he found out about the Charmeins and the more time he or Jill spent with them the less guilty he felt about his original plan of getting rid of the Charmeins and taking over the mansion. They had no family; who would miss them? They sat a few more minutes in silence and then left the truck and went into the house.

♟ ♙

The following week was strained with both of them at each other over the smallest disagreement. Sean spent several nights on the couch. A couple of nights Jill locked herself in her studio not coming out in the morning until after Sean left to go to work. One evening when Sean had to work late at the bookstore, he came home to find

Jill curled up under a blanket on the couch. Tissues were scattered on the floor which indicated a night of tears. He walked over to the couch and touched the completely covered Jill, who jumped and pulled the cover down from her red, swollen face. She looked like she had been beaten but he knew it was from crying; he had seen this face before. He softened and sitting next to her, wrapped his arms around his sad, beautiful, and talented wife. He was miserable when they weren't speaking and all the love he held inside came pouring out as he held her, especially after several days of feeling physically touch-starved.

"Babe, babe, I love you so much. I hate it when we are fighting. You know I'd do anything for you. Just tell me what, what can I do to make these tears go away?"

All she could manage were dry sobs; the tears had all come out. She snuggled up against his chest, whimpering.

Sean whispered, "Is it Noah? Is he making you crazy? I'll go talk to him and maybe give him what I should have done a while ago, a punch in the nose. Just say the word. Although he is pretty old, that punch in the nose might kill him. Or maybe that's the plan, maybe that's all I need to do, sucker punch the guy and that will end him." Jill snickered a little and he could see the hint of a smile begin to bring the light back into her face.

"No, it's not Noah. Well, it is, too. But something else. It's my show in Madison. They cancelled. I called to find out when I should bring my art. They have someone else coming in for the month. I'm not even on their schedule."

"What? You have got to be kidding me! What the fuck is going on? Are they sure, maybe they spelled your name wrong."

"They read all the names of the shows they have coming up through next year and my name was not one of them. I don't know what is going on. I don't understand why this is happening."

Sean looked up at the ceiling. Jill at first thought he was just putting his head back out of exhaustion but then she realized he was thinking about the bugs in the house.

He grabbed the paper and pen off the coffee table:

"We HAVE to stop talking in this house about ANYTHING that has to do with our work or our plans."

Jill took the paper and pen from Sean. *"I agree. But why, why would they do this to me?"*

"They want you as their maid, full-time."

"I'm not sure it is them - it really doesn't make any sense, Sean."

"It makes perfect sense - think about it. If you have a successful show, you'll have others and then you won't have time for them, to run errands and clean their huge mansion."

Jill sat quietly for a while, shaking her head, unwilling to accept that their landlord would go to such lengths. To control another person by destroying their lives and their livelihood, who does something like that? Only the most-evil people.

♟ ♙

The next morning Jill was feeling a bit more like herself again. She went up to the Charmeins and got the day's errand list. It wasn't a day of cleaning, just errands, so she planned to do more painting. But it was Sean's late night to work so they were going to lunch in Webster. She would meet him there at 11:30. He left earlier to do some of his own errands and give her time to shower and meet him at the Webster Café. As usual, Noah opened the door upon the first knock.

"Oh, good morning my dear. Well, don't you look dreadful. I hope it isn't because of the latest cancellation at the Madison Art Gallery. You shouldn't mind too much about that. I'm sure there'll be others. Here is the list for today, a short one. Don't take too long, now." He was about to close the door when he quickly added.

"One more thing, I'm sure it isn't a bother at all. We will need some raking done. If you can spare just a little of your time to start the raking before it gets out of hand. Otherwise, it will be quite a chore for you. Or perhaps Sean."

"But I thought you had a gardener."

"I was sure I told you, we had to let him go. And I had already asked you to talk to Sean about taking on that task. Please do so as soon as possible. We must get this done before it snows." And the heavy door was closed tight.

There it was, Noah knowing everything about their plans, about her cancelled show. Those damn bugs, they had to find them and rip them out. She was getting sick of the lack of privacy. And now he was demanding Sean's assistance. As if Sean had nothing to do with his time off but help take care of their gardening needs. Well, she hoped that meant they were dropping the rent even further. She showered and got ready to meet Sean for lunch.

Sean was sitting at what was sure to become 'their booth'. She waved to Dolly and joined Sean in the booth. Sean had already ordered her a cup of tea that was sitting on the table, steeping.

"I wasn't sure if a cup of tea was the right call or if you would need something stronger."

"Something stronger, but I'm not going to let those people turn me into an alcoholic."

Sean was almost afraid to ask - he was beginning to think that a punch in the nose was too mild of a punishment for Noah and wished Jill would reconsider his original plan.

"So, what is the latest with our fabulous landlords. Do tell."

Jill chuckled a little, shaking her head at the absurdity of the situation.

"Obviously they know about the cancelled show in Madison."

"What? How could they? We didn't talk about it, we wrote about it? Do they have cameras in there, too? That's it. I'm done with this."

"No, Sean. I did make the phone call when you weren't home and I was crying all by myself. I'm sure that is what they heard. And of course, I did go to his home looking 'dreadful', I believe that was the word he used."

"Isn't that nice." Sean looked down at his cup of coffee. When he looked back up, he thought he saw what he could only consider to be a look of revenge in her eyes. Maybe she was going over to the other side. He was staying clear of that topic but with the almost daily abuse the Charmeins threw their way, he was sure she would eventually come around to his way of thinking. He really hoped she would be on his side before going forward with his plan. And he was positive no one would ever find out.

"Oh yeah, I almost forgot. In your spare time, if it isn't asking too much, Noah would love it, although that wasn't his word, if you would start raking the leaves on his property. Well, he thought I would do it or perhaps you would do it."

"I thought they had a gardener."

"Well, surprise, they had to let him go, too."

"Yeah, no fuckin' way. I'm too busy running my bookstore to think about spending my free time raking and doing their gardening chores. That is a full-time job with all the land they have around their house needing maintenance." Sean thought about it for a minute and quickly reconsidered.

"Although, I did want to find a plaque or something that gave me a name, something other than Charmein. Hmm, maybe this will work. If I just tried nosing around, I could get caught. But this way, I'm raking leaves and I can look at the same time. I'll do it."

Sean had ordered a Caesar salad for Jill and a cheeseburger for him but since she was eyeing his burger, they decided to split it. She was happy with that decision and they enjoyed the shared meal.

♟ ♟

Jill did the errands for the Charmeins and when she got home, she decided she would try other art galleries. Of course, it meant driving farther away. But besides going to the gallery to show her work and then another drive to hang it and then attending the reception, she wouldn't have to be there. Hopefully she wouldn't have much to pick up when the show ended if her work sold. She needed to remain positive and just keep bringing her work to places. She still couldn't believe that the Charmeins were responsible for these galleries cancelling on her. They never leave the house, how many people could they possibly even know? They have no family. It just wasn't making sense to her. No one could have that much influence, unless you were extremely well-connected.

Chapter 9

The next day Sean didn't have to go to the bookstore until later, so he decided to explore the Charmeins' property to see if he could find any sign of a previous owner's name that he could research. He knocked on the mansion's door and waited a few minutes before Noah appeared. He seemed completely thrown off by finding Sean standing there and said so.

"Well, what are you doing here? Where is Jill?"

"She'll be here, in a bit. I heard you need a little help with the leaves. Just tell me where the rakes are and I'll see if I can take care of this for you. I only have about an hour before I have to leave for work, so..."

"Oh yes, fine, well, the rakes are in the carriage house. I'll get you the key." Noah closed the door, a bit too forcefully, in Sean's face. Seconds later he returned with one key on a key ring.

"The gardening tools are at the back of the carriage house. You'll find everything you need there." And again, the door, slammed forcefully in his face.

"Nice seeing you, too. This guy has the personality of a rock. No, a rock isn't at all annoying. How about a mosquito, yeah, that's better, a mosquito you just want to squash." Sean entertained himself by finding similarities between Noah and other annoying insects as he walked to the carriage house. He opened the lock and found a 1978 Mercedes Benz 450 SLC inside, in mint condition. Black exterior, tan leather interior. Also, a 1982 Rolls Royce, deep blue exterior and white leather interior. They both had low mileage, under 40,000 miles. He was tempted to look under the hood in each but knew they would also be pristine. He nodded his approval and continued walking to the back of the carriage house. He found the gardening tools in an enclosed section made of wire mesh. The key also worked for this room. Sean wondered why someone would feel the need to lock up their gardening tools. He found the rakes and, as he was leaving, ran his fingers down the side of the Rolls Royce. He sighed as he locked the carriage house back up. He wondered when the last time one of those two vehicles had been taken for a drive.

Back in the yard Sean started raking. He was lost in his thoughts for a while as he pictured him and Jill cruising around in the Mercedes. But then he remembered he had a purpose, and walking up towards the house, looked in the shrubs close to the front door, trying to find a name written on the stones used to build the mansion. Houses from this era often had their name along with the year the home was built on a plaque. He found nothing and after digging around the bushes and raking out a few leaves, he went back under the large oak tree, the one that was the most responsible for all the leaves. He raked the leaves into several piles. Of course, he realized he was then taking on the responsibility of getting rid of the leaves, too. He had seen a large wheelbarrow in the carriage house and went back to get that. While in there he also saw a riding mower with a leaf bag attachment. He looked at it but found it needed a key. He looked around the garden area, in a couple of obvious places someone might put a key, like on a peg board or in a drawer, but found nothing. If he was doing this again, he would definitely ask about using the mower and leaf bag. The right tools for the right job. But for now, he had a mission and decided he needed to continue looking. There was a good chance he wouldn't be helping with the raking again and he still had a lot to cover if there was any chance of finding a plaque.

He checked his watch and already a half hour had gone by. He raked vigorously feeling like he was hardly making a dent in the leaves that had fallen from the trees already. He piled some of them into the wheelbarrow and walking to the back of the yard, found a place that obviously had been used to dump leaves. He went back to rake more and was near the base of the tree when something shiny caught his eye. He walked over to the area and found something that looked a lot like a plaque partially covered by grass that had grown over it. He started digging, wishing he had a better tool than just his fingers. It was over a foot long, maybe fifteen inches, and from what he could see with how much grass he'd pulled out, there definitely appeared to be a name. He knew it was just sheer luck that he'd found the plaque. As he continued pulling grass, letters began to appear. He saw an 'n'. Ok, the Charmein name ends in 'n'. He also uncovered an 'i'. He was feeling less hopeful. But then he noticed there was another letter after the 'n', a 'g'. So, he had 'ing'. He worked harder, looking around to make sure nobody was watching him. With his luck they probably had cameras all over the property. He finished pulling out all the grass covering the plaque revealing the name: Stirling. Stirling, that sounded familiar. Directly underneath the name it said 'Manor' and the date beneath that read '1894'.

He got up and, wiping his hands on his pants and checking his time, finished up with the raking and gathered a couple more piles, taking them down to the leaf dump area. He returned the wheelbarrow and rake to the garden area, making sure to lock all doors. He ran back up to the house and knocking on the over-sized front door, waited for Noah to answer. Again, it was several minutes before he opened the door.

"Yes, what is it?" He seemed quite annoyed to be bothered.

"I'm returning your key, I have to shower and then leave for work. I didn't get much done, I'll try to do more next time, but you might want to hire someone. Or it might go faster using the leaf bag with the mower. By the way, nice rides."

"Nice what?"

"Rides, the two vehicles in the carriage house."

"The vehicles?" He seemed to not know that there were two vehicles. How could he not know?

Sean waited to see if Noah would remember the vehicles. He seemed lost in his own thoughts.

"Oh, oh, yes, the vehicles. Well, good-bye." And the door forcefully shut in his face once again.

Sean knew he had him. The Charmeins were nothing more than squatters. Another reason to take over. He was sure Jill would go along with his plan now.

♟ ♟

Jill was just getting out of the shower when Sean walked into the cottage. He washed his hands and then went to the bathroom to tell her what he'd found out. He was running a little late so had to shower fast and get out the door. But he knew he couldn't wait until later to tell her the news. He turned the shower on to muffle their voices.

"So, how did it go?" She finished drying off and was walking out of the bathroom when he took her arm and kissed her on the lips, pulling her back in the bathroom. He put his fingers to his lips indicating that they needed to whisper.

"That good, eh? So, what did you find?"

"I found a plaque, just like we thought I might. It was slightly buried and I had to dig the grass up to uncover it. But I have a name and a date."

"Really, what's the name? Not Charmein, I'm guessing." She smiled at the thought of the current residents living as thieves.

"Babe, I really want to tell you this but I have to get in the shower now. I don't have a lot of time before I have to leave."

"Well, maybe you should wait until tonight. I'll go make you a sandwich." Sean was surprised that she wasn't as curious as he would be if she'd just uncovered something this important to their whole case against the Charmeins. He decided to throw it out there and see if it sounded familiar to her. He was sure the name had to be related to the Vanderbilts somehow - more research.

"The name I found is 'Stirling'." And then he got into the shower. Jill stopped as she was buttoning her blouse and walked back into the bathroom where they could continue to whisper, hoping the shower would drown out their voices.

"Sean, what did you say?" She could hear him shampooing.

"What, the name? Yeah, it's Stirling. Does it sound familiar to you?" She couldn't believe he had forgotten so soon.

"Sean, Stirling is the homeless man in town. How do you not remember that? It was only a week or so ago." Sean stuck his head out from behind the shower curtain.

"Oh my God, Jill, you're right. The homeless guy."

"You'd better hurry. Maybe I can meet you for dinner and forget the lousy salami sandwich I was going to make you."

"Good idea. Meet me at the Café at 5pm. I'll call you if anything changes."

Sean finished his shower, dressed, and ran out the door. Jill had already left to go to the Charmeins to get her errand list for the day. Sean was bursting with his discovery and amazed that Jill had remembered that the homeless guy's name was Stirling. How could someone who obviously came from money become homeless? He realized that the Charmeins must have known about the boy's parents who were killed in a car accident, according to the story Dolly had told them, and they just moved in. And the boy was sent from institution to abusive foster home and they did nothing to protect him, just took over the house and property. What scumbags! He was sure Jill would be back on his side now. He couldn't imagine her not agreeing to go forward with his original plan.

♟ ♟

Sean was itching at work all day, anxious to meet Jill for dinner and continue their conversation from this morning. He was having a hard time staying focused and his employee, Brenda, noticed.

"What's up, Sean, you seen really distracted today? You feeling ok?" Brenda was a matronly woman in her early fifties who loved the role of mothering everyone. Jennie, his other employee who was just into her twenties, actually called her 'mum' and said Brenda was like the mother she'd never had. Jennie had some family issues and lived with a cousin who worked in town. They were good employees and Sean felt lucky to have them both.

"I'm good, just a lot going on at home. Maybe I'll tell you about it someday." Brenda waited but Sean went back to his order form. They were having a good month and he was stocking up for the holiday season which was just around the corner. He smiled at Brenda and although she was hesitant to move, giving Sean the chance to convey something more to her, he did not and she finally left the desk where he was working. Fortunately, a customer came into the shop so she walked over to see if she could assist them.

Sean was relieved that someone had come in the shop to distract Brenda. He was bursting to tell someone about what he'd uncovered with the Charmeins and feared he might open up to Brenda or even a complete stranger. He knew that would put the whole operation in jeopardy and could throw both him and Jill in jail. He had to keep everything to himself. He hoped Jill was the same but since she was not working at the school anymore, he knew there weren't many people she was in contact with other than the Charmeins.

Fortunately, Sean kept busy and the day flew by. He left the store at 4:30 to meet Jill at the Café. He parked and was walking towards the Café when he saw the man in the red parka. He stopped to look at him, wondering if he should approach him.

"Stirling?" The man turned and, looking frightened that this strange man knew his name, took off running.

"Well, that went well." Sean walked into the Café and saw Jill sitting in their booth. It was a little busier than usual. She had a glass of white wine in front of her and a black coffee for Sean.

"Hey, why do I get coffee?"

"Because you have to go back to work."

"Yeah, but you have to drive home."

"I don't think one glass of wine is going to prevent me from driving home. Especially when I get a bowl of tomato soup and a grilled cheese sandwich."

"Yum." Jill knew he was being sarcastic - he didn't care for tomato soup. And he only had a grilled cheese sandwich for breakfast."

"So, what are you having?"

Dolly came over and as usual, gave Sean a big smile.

"How are you today, Dolly?"

"Well, hello Sean. I'm just fine. Your wife already ordered but she had no idea what you wanted so waited for you. Do you know what you want?"

He looked over the menu and then chose the meatloaf with mashed potatoes and green beans.

"I'm in the mood for some comfort food."

Dolly agreed. "That'll do it!" She walked away and gave their orders to the cook. Sean watched her walk away and then turned to Jill, grabbing her hands that were folded in front of her on the table. She jumped a little, surprised at his energy.

"What? Is this about the information you had to share this morning?"

"Yes, yes, don't you know what this means?"

"Yeah, I do. It means the Charmeins are assholes. It means they somehow got the mansion away from this boy and he was sent to institutions and abused. It breaks my heart."

"Speaking of the boy, he was lingering outside when I walked up. I said his name and he took off running."

"You shouldn't bother him, Sean. He sounds harmless from what Dolly said but you just don't know. He could attack you if he feels threatened."

"I said his name, that is hardly a threat."

"Ok, well, back to your story. What else do you have to share?"

"So, I went to the carriage house to get the rakes. It's like a warehouse it's so huge. There's a Rolls Royce and a Mercedes in there. Both in mint condition. And when I mentioned the vehicles to Noah, he didn't seem to know what the hell I was talking about! How can you not know you have two classic cars in your own garage? And in such immaculate condition?"

"Well, like they said, they are mostly house-bound. They don't get out much so have no need for vehicles. I can see that." Her lack of enthusiasm was antithesis to Sean's bursting energy. She seemed distracted. He was hoping she was on the same page as him and would be ready to move forward with the plan.

"What's up, Babe? Have something on your mind?"

"Yeah, I guess I do. I called the school. They didn't make a decision but had two people they were deciding between. And I wasn't one of them."

"Great, that just confirms that you aren't supposed to be a teacher. You're supposed to be an artist and live in a big mansion with twenty rooms surrounded by master artworks." She knew he was trying to cheer her up and managed a weak smile.

"Here we are. Sean, your comfort food. And Jill, your diet food. Well, that's what diet food looks like to me. But I know you'll enjoy it. You let me know if you need anything else, ok?" Dolly walked away with the serving tray.

"Yeah, but until that happens, in the meantime, I feel like we're struggling."

Sean lit up. That definitely sounded like agreement to him and he decided to push forward.

"By the way, I found the perfect poison." He kept his voice low.

"You did?"

"Yes, and I'll do everything, you don't have to do a thing, unless you want to make the dessert. I'll do the rest."

"Ok." They ate the rest of their meal in silence. Sean paid and they left the Café. He pulled her to him and hugged her hard.

"I love you so much, babe. You know I would never do anything to hurt you. I only want the best for us. You know that, right?"

Jill nodded, kissed him on the cheek, and turned to leave.

"Sean, did you contact a realtor about an apartment?"

"Yes, I did. They had nothing, would call us if something came in but there aren't many apartments available in the area. We would have to drive to Madison, which is more than 40 miles away.

"Ok, bye." He couldn't stand seeing her this depressed and knew they had to act now before she changed her mind.

♟ ♙

Your presence is requested at the home of
Noah and Charlotte Charmein.
The occasion: Dinner and drinks
Date: Sunday, November 17
Time: 6:30pm
Dinner will be served promptly at 7pm
after drinks and hors d'oeuvres in the parlor.
Dessert and coffee will follow dinner
after a short rest in the parlor.
We request that you arrive on time.

Jill's hands shook as she took the invitation from the envelope. She knew this was it. This was the start of what could be the end for her and Sean, if it all didn't go according to Sean's plan. Her stomach lurched and she thought she would lose her dinner. She couldn't help shaking and poured herself a glass of wine. She paced the floor sipping her wine, waiting for Sean to come home. She lay down on the couch with a washcloth on her forehead and fell asleep.

Chapter 10

They dressed as usual but this time Jill wore a sweater - she knew from spending more time at the Charmeins, when she went there to clean, that it was usually quite cool with the high ceilings and marble floors. Of course, the dining room and parlor where they visited would most likely be warm enough but she had a chill she couldn't get rid of and felt better with a sweater. Sean carried the fruit pie he'd made and a bottle of champagne. Noah was there to greet them at the first knock on the door.

"What's this?" He reached for the bottle of champagne but eyed the dessert suspiciously.

"Well," Jill started, "your invitations always say 'dessert and coffee' but since we haven't yet had a dessert, I thought we should bring one."

"Oh, isn't that sweet of you. Charley is very particular so I'll let her decide if she wants to keep this."

They walked into the mansion, following close behind Noah, into the parlor, still carrying the dessert. Charley sat in her usual chaise lounge, sipping the familiar champagne.

"My dear, the people here brought us a dessert. Whatever should we do with it?"

Charley looked at the dessert they were holding and, with a look of disgust on her face, pointed to the kitchen.

"Just put it in there, I suppose. Thank you so much. That was very kind." Her fake graciousness was about as syrupy sweet as the fruit pie. Sean looked at Jill who had a slightly worried look on her face. He got her attention and, smiling, gave her a wink.

Noah took the pie from them as if they had instead brought a pie made with roadkill. Sean noticed the look and smiled to himself, knowing they would have at least as nauseous a face if they knew what was really in the pie. He sat down next to Jill and they engaged in their usual empty chit-chat with the Charmeins.

Jill took a long sip of her champagne which brought Noah to his feet so he could refill her glass.

"Oh, thank you." And she took another long sip.

"Oh my, you should be careful you don't drink too much - you might get sick. Oh dear, we forgot the hors d'oeuvres. I do apologize. We were so busy preparing the meal tonight we just forgot all about our usual pre-dinner snack. Well, let's just relax a few minutes and then we'll go in to dinner. We certainly don't want you drinking too much on an empty stomach. Do we Charley?"

"Oh, good heavens, no! There is nothing worse than a hangover. And I've had a few in my life. Just dreadful. Maybe we could give her some crackers. Would you like some crackers, dear?"

Jill forced a smile.

"No, I'm fine, I'll be fine. But thank you."

Sean swore he saw her lip curl. He knew how much Jill hated phony shows of caring. But it seems the Charmeins just couldn't help themselves.

"So, how is your painting going?" Charley smiled, holding her champagne glass up for a refill.

"Fine." Jill's curtness didn't seem to faze Charley at all. She continued to admire her champagne, appearing hypnotized by the bubbles. Sean noticed Jill was also staring into her own glass of champagne.

"That's nice. And how is the other one?" Noah leaned down to Charley and you could hear him whisper in her ear, 'Sean'.

"Ah, Sean, yes, don't you read books?"

"Well, actually, I sell them and yes I do read them but I'm also writing a novel."

"Oh, good for you. For all that."

Noah seemed a little anxious about something as if he wanted the night to get on with itself. Or he had another appointment. Or he was waiting for more guests to arrive. Something was causing him to pace more than usual and look at his watch. Which surprised Sean because he wondered why either of them would even need a watch since they stayed in all day. He didn't even think they had a TV, unless there was one in the bedroom. He remembered Jill saying that Charley's room was off limits - maybe she actually sat around all day eating bon-bons and watching soaps but didn't want anyone to know that. Sean decided to be bold, although he didn't want to offend either of them. He remembered what happened the last time Jill had asked a personal question. And he wanted to be sure they at least tried the fruit pie they'd brought.

"Are you waiting for someone, Noah?" Noah jumped slightly and actually giggled.

"No, no, why do you ask?"

"Well, you keep checking your watch. I thought maybe you were expecting someone."

Noah quickly composed himself.

"If you must know, we're trying something new, heated dinner plates, and I want to be sure our food isn't getting cold. Perhaps we should go in to dinner."

"Well, that's a wonderful idea, my dear. We don't want her getting sick from too much champagne." And

Noah stood next to Charley as she grabbed his arm and walked to the dining room.

Jill and Sean followed behind them. Jill also took Sean's arm and found herself feeling a bit dizzy. She stumbled but Sean caught her. They were both sure the Charmeins didn't notice and continued to their seats in the dining room. Sean eyed Jill with a questioning look - she put up a hand to indicate she was fine. No need to worry about her. He pulled out her chair and she very carefully sat down.

The plates already had their food on them.

"We bought these plate warmers and wanted to see if they actually worked. You are certainly more than welcome to help yourself to more food if you are still hungry after this meal. Or maybe you want to save room for dessert, which we also made tonight. Our apologies for not having dessert the last couple of times but if you remember, Sean, your wife was a bit rude to my Charley last time. But we are hoping to forget all that and so we made a nice apple cobbler, if you want. And we will certainly put your dessert out as well, if you prefer that."

Surprising to both Sean and Jill, their meals were still hot, as if they had just been served. Tonight's meal was roast pork, red baked potatoes, and butternut squash. There was also a basket of rolls, wrapped in a cloth and still warm. Noah poured them each more champagne, giving Jill just a half glass. She gave him dagger eyes which he didn't catch.

"Well, bon appetit." Charley raised her glass. They each raised their glasses and drank.

The food, as usual, was delicious. Sean finished his and was looking for more of the roast pork in the chafing dishes in the middle of the table. He was just lifting the cover when the door to the dining room opened. Sean and Jill both jumped since they were positive there was no one else in the mansion. Jill never saw anyone when she came here to clean and the Charmeins themselves never spoke of having company. Even though Noah told Jill they sometimes had company, she still believed he was just trying to throw her off and that he was the only one who'd used the two rooms that she'd cleaned and changed the bedding in a few times. Since Charley had her room and Noah never pointed out that any one particular room was his, she continued to believe that he just slept in whatever room he wanted. But now, here was someone coming into the room while they were eating.

Sean and Jill both looked at the Charmeins to see their reaction. They seemed pleased and, smiling, barely acknowledged the man who simply walked through the room and out another door without stopping to talk. When he had left, Charley finally spoke.

"Oh, that's cousin Drew." And she and Noah continued eating. Sean and Jill looked at each other and Jill mouthed 'homeless man'. Sean nodded.

Cousin Drew? Sean was positive he and Jill were told the Charmeins had no living relatives. Now they meet the homeless man and are told that he is their cousin? If he is a Stirling, and the castle was owned by the Stirling family, why isn't cousin Drew living here instead of the Charmeins? And who are the Charmeins to the Stirling family? Sean thought more than ever that the Charmeins were just squatters, which is why he had been unable to find out anything about them.

After dinner they moved back to the parlor and Noah left to bring in the apple cobbler dessert that the Charmeins had made. Coffee was brewing on the side table and Noah raised the pot to pour them each a cup.

"Do we all want coffee?" Sean raised a finger, Jill shook her head no and Charley raised her champagne glass.

"So, just two. Fine. And I'll cut the apple cobbler, two pieces. One for each of you."

"Where's the dessert we brought?" Jill wondered why Noah hadn't also brought their dessert in.

"Oh, would you like some of that my dear?" Noah moved to go towards the kitchen.

"Well, no, we made it for you, if you want a piece. I am quite full, so doubt I will eat more than a bite or two." Jill sipped her champagne. Noah moved to fill her glass but she put her hand over the top of the glass.

"Had enough, have you? Yes, we do have errands for you tomorrow so I'd hate for you to have a headache in the morning."

"Aren't you having any of your apple cobbler?" Jill was feeling brave and wanted to get the niceties out of the way so she could find out more about Stirling – cousin Drew – and what he was doing in their home.

"So, the man who walked through. You said he's your cousin? We saw a man in town who was dressed like him and we heard his name is Stirling. We understood he didn't drive and wasn't a fully functioning adult, if you know what I mean. How did he get here?"

Noah put the knife down loudly on the counter where he stood cutting the cobbler. They all turned to look at him.

"My dear, are you really going to insult us another time by questioning why we are giving shelter to our cousin? And, furthermore, insulting a relative of ours by questioning his mental abilities? You really should watch your tongue. And perhaps, young man, you need to control your wife a bit more." Sean looked from Noah to Jill who was now turning darker shades of red before his eyes.

"I do not ever control my wife. She speaks her mind. And, I have to agree with her, how did someone who has no vehicle make his way to your humble abode? And, cousin? I thought you had no relatives, that is what we were told by the realtor. No children, no family. And now a cousin shows up and we were told in town that he'd lost his parents and was sent from institution to foster homes where he was abused."

Noah was getting riled and they could tell he wasn't going to take much more.

"The young man you are talking about is no relation to us. You are confusing him with the man who is staying at our home. That is cousin Drew. I do not know anyone named 'Stirling.' And now, once again, I think you both need to leave. I do wish we could have a pleasant meal without all of your insults. It is so upsetting to Charley, you have no idea." Sean and Jill turned to Charley who was lounging once again on her chaise lounge, her head back, her eyes closed, champagne glass ready to slip out of her hand. Noah, noticing this, quickly grabbed the glass before it crashed to the floor. He then turned and walked to the front door, opened it, and waited for Sean and Jill to leave.

♟ ♟

Back in the cottage, Sean and Jill were so wound up. They couldn't believe the Charmeins and the lies they were throwing at them. Jill poured them each a glass of wine and they sat on the couch, too upset to relax. It was only 9:30 and too early for either of them to go to bed. Jill considered getting her frustrations out on the canvas. But she knew she'd most likely have to gesso over the canvas because nothing positive would come from coming in her present state of mind. She really was not in a positive mood at all. She was steaming but Sean had to speak first.

"Can you believe them?" He stopped and pointed to the ceiling. They were aware that they were being listened to and so they'd have to take it outside. Being unable to speak freely was just so frustrating, but it was too late to go to the café where they were able to have normal conversations without having to whisper or write everything on paper. They put their coats on and, with wine glasses in hand, walked out the front door and got into Sean's truck. He started it so they could have some heat.

"As I was saying, they must think we are really stupid. That was Stirling, was it not? Same red jacket, same grease and dirt-stained pants. It was him. And Noah is saying it is not him, that we're mistaken. We saw Stirling in town. They just used him tonight. They are pretending they have a relative. I don't know how they know, but I think they know what we are planning. And, if we think they have family, we won't do anything to them. Doesn't it seem that way to you?"

Jill was listening but felt a dizziness come over her. She thought maybe she did have a little too much to drink and put the wine glass down on the dashboard.

"Are you ok, babe?"

"Yeah, just felt a little dizzy. I think I had too much to drink. Maybe we can continue this tomorrow. You have an early day, right? Maybe we can meet at the

Café again. But yeah, that was definitely Stirling. No one would wear exactly the same clothes as a homeless man, I mean they were dirty and soiled just like the ones Stirling was wearing. But you see, they didn't know that we saw him in town. That we know he isn't a relative. Anyway, I have to cut this short, Sean. I need to lie down."

"How about some coffee? Or maybe just drink lots of water. Do we have any Alka-Seltzer? You should drink fluids if it is a hangover coming on."

"Ok, I will." Jill left the cab and stumbled a little going up the stairs.

"Do you need some help, Babe?" He started to reach for her but she held up a hand, waved him away, and went into the house. Sean went back to his truck and finished his wine. He couldn't stop thinking about what had transpired tonight. Either the Charmeins were crazy or he was crazy and he was pretty sure he wasn't crazy. He didn't know how much he and Jill could take. All of his hope was in the fruit pie. What if they didn't eat it? What would they do then? He didn't know how else to get the poison to them. Then he remembered that Jill got meds for Charley. Maybe they could add a couple of home-made pills to the mix. But who knew how often Charley even took the meds - it could be months before she took any. And then that would just take care of Charley. What would they do about Noah? He needed to come up with another plan. In the meantime, he wanted to do some research on the name Stirling. It sounded like a last name and hopefully he could find something when he searched on the name at the library.

Chapter 11

The next morning when Sean got up the bed on Jill's side was empty. He thought she must have gone to the Charmeins earlier than usual but then he heard her in the bathroom. He opened the door and found her with her head over the bowl.

"Babe, are you ok? What can I do for you? I'll get you some water." He started to leave for the kitchen when Jill grabbed his leg. She slid to the floor, put her elbows on her knees, and held her head between her hands.

"Stay, please." He squatted on the floor next to her and put his hand on her calf. She was crying.

"What can I do?" He had seen her hungover before but never like this.

"Is there something else going on? Do you think you have a virus?"

"Or a case of pregnancy?" She tried to smile but instead a moan came out.

"Pregnant? That's impossible. You're on birth control." Sean knew this was not a good time for her to be pregnant and although he would be thrilled to have a baby with Jill, he hoped it wasn't happening now.

"I am, but they don't always work."

"Right. Well, do you want to go to the doctor? Or we can just do a pregnancy test."

"We have a winner - pregnancy test. But, let's not rush to any conclusions."

"Ok, I'll pick one up. Do you want me to go to the Charmeins? I can do their damn errands."

"No, just give me a minute. If I can't move by the time you shower, you can pick up their list and then I'll get to it later. If I can't, I'll call you and tell you what they want. Deal?"

He smiled at her sensibleness.

"Deal!" And he hopped in the shower. When he came out Jill wasn't on the floor but he found her on the bed, sleeping. He dressed and then went to the Charmeins to pick up the list.

Noah was back to his usual cheerful self and since they were speaking freely in the cottage despite the bugs, opened the door and simply handed the list to Sean.

"I hope your wife feels better. Send my best." And promptly closed the heavy door with a loud bang.

"God-damned bugs!" Sean stuck up his middle finger at the double doors and walked back to the cottage. He was hoping to find Jill up but she was still in bed, covers over her head. He kissed the top of her head that stuck out from the covers and left for work, leaving the list on the kitchen table. He decided he would visit the library during his lunch break and see if he could find anything on the name Stirling.

Sean couldn't get into his work and of course, again, Brenda noticed.

"How are you doing today, Sean?"

"I don't know, I don't feel quite right, bit of an upset stomach, you know. Must have been something I ate." He thought that would satisfy Brenda but it did not.

"Something you ate? You just seem distracted, that's all. Like you have something on your mind." Brenda waited, expecting Sean to spill his guts. Of course, with how his stomach was feeling he might literally spill his guts.

"No, no, just stomach upset. Nothing else, really. Lots on my mind, too. The business, you know."

"Ok, just checking." And she went back to stocking the shelves on the non fiction books.

Around 1pm Sean hadn't heard from Jill so decided to call her. He was hoping she would feel better by now, fully recovered from her hangover if that's what it was. The phone rang several times but she never picked up. He left a message, asking her to call him when she got up. He didn't have the list so couldn't shop for the Charmeins. He knew he should have taken the list with him.

At lunch, Sean left the bookstore and headed for the library. The same pleasant librarian was there and he asked to use one of the computers. She gave him a clipboard to sign up to use it and he sat down to start his research on Stirling.

There was a lot of information on a city in Scotland that was called Stirling. And there was a castle. Interesting, he thought. The name Stirling was ancient and the castle itself was many centuries old. The castle had changed hands about 8 times in 50 years, having once been home to Mary Queen of Scots and King James VI. Another interesting fact was that the name Stirling came from 'striveling' meaning place of strife which was fitting, he read, for a town that was witness to gory murders, long sieges, and bloody battles.

Sean wasn't satisfied that this was what he was looking for but it was a step in the right direction. The fact that there was a Stirling Castle and he found the plaque that said Stirling Manor all made sense to him. There was definitely a connection there somewhere.

He did a little more research and found a Stirling that was, indeed, connected to the Vanderbilts. That intrigued him and he knew he would have to take another trip to the library to see what else he could find on that connection.

On his way back to the bookstore he decided to call Jill again. Still no answer. Hopefully she was in the shower. He would try again later.

Around 4pm, when he still hadn't heard from Jill, he called again. Finally, she picked up the phone.

"Hello?"

"Babe, I've been calling you all afternoon. How are you feeling?"

"Like shit. If this is a hangover it's the worst one I've ever had. When I've had other hangovers, I just feel it in my stomach – I just want the food out. But this one I feel in my whole body."

"So, do you want me to pick up that pregnancy test? Do you think that is a possibility?"

"Well, if it is I'm suing the bastards who make the birth control pills."

"Could you have missed taking one?"

"Not a chance, I never forget."

"Ok, so, do you want me to pick up a test or just some Pepto Bismol or even ibuprofen, if you think it is hangover related.

"Yeah, get the Pepto, ibuprofen – just get everything. This is dreadful, Sean. I just want to lie in bed. I did get up and shower but I just have dry heaves now. I don't have anything in me, even the water comes up."

"Look, you could become dehydrated. You should drink some broth or do we have any Gatorade? You need electrolytes. You could become seriously ill. You need to take care of yourself. Don't just sleep, try to eat something."

Jill was getting impatient – he could tell she wanted to hang up.

"I keep throwing up, I don't want to eat anything. I'll see if we have Gatorade. I have to go, Sean."

"Wait, the list, give me their damned errand list."

Jill read off the few items on the list and then after giving him a quick 'bye' hung up the phone.

He was really worried about her and couldn't focus anymore at work. He knew he had to leave to take care of his wife. Since Brenda and Jennie were both on the late shift that night, at 4:30pm he told them he was leaving early. Of course, Brenda was fine with it, concern showing on her face.

Sean left and did the few errands for the Charmeins. Their list consisted of picking up food items at the grocery store. He couldn't remember if they had Gatorade at home so he picked up a few bottles and the powder mix. He also got Jill a pregnancy test and a couple of different medications for nausea. He left for home and when he got there, she was still in bed. He knew this was something more and although he didn't want to wake her, he did.

"Hey, how are you feeling?" He held a bottle of Gatorade in his hand.

"Better. But I'm really hungry." He handed her the Gatorade and she drank it down. He noticed how pale she looked and was about to suggest they take a ride to the hospital when she suddenly got up. She was a little unsteady on her feet and Sean grabbed her arm to help her. She smiled and, leaning on him, they walked to the bathroom. He gave her privacy although he wanted to hold her. He felt so protective of her always but even more so when she was sick.

"Could you make me a scrambled egg? And a dry piece of toast?"

"Of course. I also got you some Pepto and ibuprofen, if you need that. But I'll make you a plain scrambled egg and dry toast, coming up."

He was happy she wanted food but still worried that a hangover could last so long. But, if it wasn't a hangover, could it have been something she ate? He'd eaten the same things, though, and although his stomach was a little off, it was nothing like what Jill was experiencing. Sean suddenly thought about how their food had already been on the plates and made a mental note to mention this to Jill the next time they could talk in private. Then again, it just might have been one hell of a hangover.

♟ ♟

The next morning Sean reached for Jill and found her side of the bed empty. He jumped out of bed, hoping he wouldn't find a similar scene to yesterday with Jill curled up around the toilet bowl. He opened the bathroom door but she wasn't there. He walked into the kitchen and found her sitting at the table, dressed, with coffee and breakfast made. He smiled and walked over to plant a kiss on the top of her head.

"I can't tell you how happy I am to see you looking more like yourself again."

Jill smiled and patted the seat next to her, inviting him to sit. She also pointed to the ceiling, just a subtle reminder that someone was listening. She had a pad and pencil next to her ready to write their conversation:

"*We need to talk - I'm concerned that they might not eat our dessert.*" Jill pushed the pad of paper to Sean as he sipped his coffee and ate his English muffin with peanut butter.

"*Yes! I agree, thinking the same thing. Do you have any ideas?*"

"*Make brownies, peace offering?*"

"*Ok, but how does that help our cause?*" Sean was a little confused. He didn't see how making more desserts would do the job.

Jill took the paper and pencil and wrote:

"*They might see this as something different than regular dessert, if they were suspicious about our dinner dessert. And I could bring it when I went to clean, which is tomorrow. They may even eat it right in front of me, while I'm cleaning.*"

"*Ok, I see where your thinking is going. By the way, maybe we should write this on my computer. I can type faster.*"

"*I know, I thought of that, too, but I like burning the paper notes because then there's no trace of our conversations. I just don't trust the computer - even if we deleted it, I fear it could show up somewhere. Just being paranoid.*"

Sean knew she was right and shared her paranoia. He finished breakfast and hopped in the shower. When he was dressed and ready to go, she stood at the door holding his bagged lunch. He grabbed her around the waist pulling her close to him and whispered in her ear.

"I don't know what I'd do without you, babe. I love you so much." Jill kissed his neck and they kissed, holding each other as if they would both die if either let go. He finally let her go and left before he changed his mind and called in sick. Except he knew he couldn't do that; it was, after all, his bookstore. Jill held the door open a crack and threw him kisses as he drove away.

The day was fairly normal for both of them. Sean was more relaxed at work now that Jill was feeling better and after Jill picked up Noah's list and did the errands, remembering to buy some brownie mix, she actually did a little painting in her studio. When Sean came home, she had a roast chicken with red potatoes cooking in the oven. Frozen peas and carrots were cooking on the stove. The smell was warm and inviting when Sean walked through the door.

"Perfect, and I have just the complement to your amazing meal." He brought out a bottle of nice red cabernet.

"Ah, I think I need a few days without alcohol." Jill smiled and grimaced at the same time.

"Oh, yeah, right. I forgot, sorry." Sean put the wine down on the counter. Then he put his finger to his lips and mouthed the words 'brownies'. Jill nodded.

"*All ready for your finishing touches.*" She scribbled on the notepad sitting next to her on the table.

They ate their delicious meal in silence. Sean skipped the wine and they each had a big glass of ice water. They held hands, Sean stopping occasionally to kiss Jill's hand. After supper Jill cleared the dishes from the table and Sean finished the brownies, popping them in the oven. When they were done Jill cut them and layered them onto a plate covering the brownies with plastic wrap.

Of course, neither of them slept much. They talked, in whispers, about the mansion and how wonderful it would be to live there. They held each other through the night and when they woke, they were still wrapped together. They made love, in silence, biting down on a pillow at the moment of climax. Time stood still for the few more minutes they lay in the bed until Sean finally dragged himself away. Jill fell back to sleep and after he showered and dressed, he left her sleeping and slipped out the door and off to work.

When Jill got up, showered, and ate breakfast, she was surprised that it was already 9:30. Then she remembered the brownies. Her stomach felt queasy but this time it wasn't from a hangover but from nerves. She debated calling Sean for support but she knew he was busy at work. She had to do this herself.

She arrived at the Charmeins' door holding the brownies with both hands. She briefly considered tossing them behind the bushes near the front door. As usual she didn't wait long before Noah flung the door open.

"Well good morning my dear, and what have we here? Did you bring something for us to eat, again?"

"Yes. Yes, I did. It's my attempt at making amends and to tell you how sorry we are about everything. You were right, I had too much to drink and I felt awful for a couple of days. I didn't put any walnuts in because I didn't know if you or Charley were allergic, some people are and I didn't know. But anyway, here they are and I hope you enjoy them. If you like them, let me know and I'll make you another batch. Or, if you don't like brownies, I can make something else?" Jill stopped because she realized she was rambling and didn't want Noah to be suspicious of her behavior. He was looking at her through narrow eyes, waiting for her to stop. She felt her face warming up and handed the plate to Noah. He didn't take the plate but turned and led her to the kitchen and pointed to the counter for her to put them on.

"You are here to clean today, correct? So, I'll let you tend to that now." And he turned and walked away. Jill took a few minutes to compose herself and found her hands were shaking. She splashed some cold water on her face and after drying with a paper towel, found the dust cloth and other cleaning products and headed upstairs to the bedrooms.

She again found two of the rooms, the same two rooms, had been used so she changed the sheets and took a little more time on dusting and cleaning their bathrooms. She walked through the other bedrooms and finding them spotless, lightly wiped the furniture down with the dust cloth. The bathrooms were spotless, so she left them as they were. And then she found herself just outside Charley's room. She was more than curious about the room and why it was off-limits. As she had told Sean when she'd bought morphine for Charley, perhaps she had cancer and her days were numbered. But she couldn't be sure. She pressed her ear against the door hoping to hear talking or the sounds of someone who was quite ill. She knew what that sounded like since she was so sick herself just a few days ago. She started to move her hand toward the doorknob, not knowing what she would do when she opened the door and even more unsure of what she might find inside. Suddenly, the door was opened just enough for Noah to squeeze out. But still, she saw nothing.

"What are you doing? I told you not to ever bother Charley."

"I'm sorry, I finished the dusting and just need to vacuum and mop the kitchen but I was wondering if I could make you some coffee that you could have with the brownies. I would be happy to do that for you."

Again, the narrow eyes. And then he brightened.

"Oh, splendid. Yes, please do. Charley and I will be down momentarily. But first, finish the vacuuming and oh, also, I have a list for you as well." He handed her the list and she put it in her jeans pocket.

Noah went back into Charley's room and Jill ran down the stairs. She found the vacuum and after running it over the two used rooms put the coffee on. She found cups and saucers and little plates for their brownies. She poured herself a little coffee but obviously she wasn't going to have any brownies. She thought about this, how could she get away with giving them the brownies and not having any herself? Allergic to chocolate? Can't eat sugar? Doesn't like brownies? She wasn't that good of a liar. And then she thought, she had to go do the errands because she was meeting Sean for a late lunch. Yes, that was it. She wanted to get out of the house as soon as possible and that should do it.

When she finished the cleaning and put everything away, she brought the plate of brownies into the parlor and set out the two cups of coffee. She decided to not even have a coffee which would prove her point that she really was in a hurry. Then she went back into the kitchen and mopped. When she came out Charley and Noah were sitting in the parlor in their usual spots, with Charley on the chaise lounge chair and Noah standing next to the coffee pot and plate of brownies.

"That was sweet that you put a brownie on each of our plates and poured our coffee. But I don't see your coffee or your brownie." Charley somehow looked odd to Jill and then she realized, she wasn't holding a glass of champagne. Jill felt her heart pounding in her chest and was sure they could hear it and would know that she'd done something to the brownies. She felt her face warming up but tried to stay cool.

"Oh, yes, I'm sorry. I forgot Sean and I made plans to meet for a late lunch. I have to go back to the cottage and shower and drive to his store in Lebron. We usually meet in Webster but he can't today, he can't take that much time so we have to meet in Lebron where his bookstore is. So, I don't have a lot of time, I have to get ready. But I'll bring some more brownies next time, if you like them. This was just a way of making amends." Jill stopped suddenly. She was rambling again.

Charley and Noah exchanged looks. Jill felt her hands shaking and then Charley looked at her with a dead-eye stare.

"But we insist." Her words were so convincing that Jill almost sat in the chair waiting for Noah to bring her coffee and a brownie. But she didn't. She wouldn't let them intimidate her. She knew she had to run.

"Sorry, but I have to go." And she ran out the parlor door to the front door, pulling it closed behind her and slamming it shut. She ran all the way to the cottage.

Chapter 12

Jill hopped in the shower and, although she had locked all the doors, kept hearing sounds outside the bathroom. She was convinced she'd been followed. She kept peeking around the curtain while rushing to finish. She dried off and quickly dressed, dialing Sean's number as she got into her car. She'd made sure to put Noah's list in her purse and drove directly to Sean's bookstore.

When the bell rang over the door announcing someone had entered, Sean did a double-take. He was quite surprised to see Jill. He walked over to her and gave her a hug.

"What are you doing here? I certainly wasn't expecting this. Did you bring me lunch?"

Brenda waved and Jill waved back at her.

"Is there someplace we can go to talk in private?" She didn't want to discuss anything to do with the Charmeins where other people might hear.

"Sure, we'll go into my office. Let me know if you need any help, Brenda."

"I'll be fine." Brenda watched them walk into the back room and then turned back to straightening the book shelves.

"What's going on babe?" Jill wrapped her arms around Sean and didn't want to let go. She felt a weight had been taken off her and, suddenly feeling weak, she sat down in his chair. He pulled another chair up beside her and held both of her hands in his.

"Just take it slow. Do you want some water, or we can make you some tea, I think we have some herbals." Jill shook her head and took a deep breath.

"So, I brought them the brownies and I did my cleaning and I told them I would make coffee for them to go with the brownies. And when I finished the cleaning, I had everything set up and... they wanted me to join them."

"Well, of course you wouldn't. But yeah, that might have looked suspicious to them. Damn, I didn't think about that. Maybe we should just bring something for them and leave it there and not suggest they eat it right away."

"Sean, they both insisted. If you could see the looks on their faces. I was terrified. For one second, I thought they would hold me down and force feed me the brownie. It was like they knew."

Sean let go of her hands and sat back in the chair.

"Hmm, yeah, I guess it could appear that way to them. So the next time we bring them some dessert and, like I said, we just leave it. Or I have an even better idea. We bring them dessert and we eat it, too."

"What? Are you crazy?"

"No, listen, this is brilliant. We bring an untainted dessert, which we will eat, and then when we bring another one it will have the poison. Which, of course, we won't eat. But since we ate one with them, they won't have any reason to suspect we are going to poison the next one. They might even think they are being paranoid."

Jill jumped off the chair and sat on Sean's lap.

"You're right, you are brilliant. That's a great plan. Good. But do we have to wait until we go to their house for dinner again? There has to be another reason to visit before that. This is just dragging out way too long now."

Sean thought back to Jill's reaction when he first floated the idea of poisoning the Charmeins and was surprised by her complete one-eighty of wanting to put his latest idea into action without delay.

"We just have to be patient, ok? So, how about I take you to lunch now?" Jill sighed and, taking Sean's hand, they walked out of the bookstore together.

♟ ♟

After lunch, Sean went back to the store and Jill did her errands. When she returned home, she was tempted to knock on the Charmeins' door, leave their items, and just run. But it was getting colder out now and there were a couple of items that might freeze. She did keep her distance when Noah opened the door, imagining that he would reach over, grab her hand, drag her into the house, and shove a brownie down her throat. She handed the bag to Noah and was about to turn and leave when he spoke up.

"Oh, dear, could you please tell your husband that we really need the leaves raked now. It is turning colder and most of them have fallen from the trees so he needs to clean them up. He has only been here once. But now with winter upon us, we may soon have snow and we can't have this mess. As soon as possible."

Jill was surprised, first, that they seem to have forgotten their names. And second, that Noah seemed to think that Sean worked for him and Charley now.

"I'm sorry, but Sean did it that one time for you as a favor, but since he doesn't work for you, he really doesn't have time to clean your property. You have too much land. It would be a full-time job for him. So, you'll have to hire someone, find a new gardener."

"Oh, I see. So, he found what he was looking for that time, did he?" Jill felt herself blush. She was sure they hadn't talked about looking for a plaque at the cottage and wondered how he could know that. She decided instead to react defensively.

"He wasn't looking for anything. He was being a good tenant and helping you out until you found a new gardener. Maybe you should be more grateful." She had no idea where this boldness was coming from but she took another step back from the door.

Noah stood staring at her, nodding his head, sizing her up. She often felt like he could see right through her and into her mind to read her thoughts.

"Yes, well, fine. We'll see about that." And he slammed the massive door in her face.

Back at the cottage Jill took notes on the confrontation between her and Noah; she wanted Sean to know exactly what had happened. She had no idea what Noah meant by 'we'll see about that' but she thought she should tell Sean so he could be fully aware. It certainly sounded like a threat to her.

That night when Sean arrived home Jill came out of the cottage and, getting into the truck, directed Sean to take a little ride. She told him what Noah had said and shared her feelings that it sounded like a threat. Sean wasn't as ruffled.

"Well, I'm beginning to see through this guy. He likes to act like a big deal, but they're probably as suspicious of us as we are of them. Even though Charley is obviously as bad as Noah, you know he's the one who's listening to our conversations, insults us, bosses us around, tries to control us, and treats us like we're their hired help."

"I don't know, you didn't see the look I got from both of them when they were trying to get me to eat the brownies. She had a look I'll never forget. Pure evil."

"I'm guessing since he seemed fine, they probably didn't eat the brownies. I'm not going to worry about it. I think we should move forward with our new plan - we'll make an edible dessert and both eat it to show them it's ok and that we're not trying to poison them. And then, the next time, bring another dessert laced with enough poison to put them both out of their misery."

"Ok, but how do we get out of eating the poisoned dessert?"

"That's easy, we'll just say something to offend them so they'll throw us out just like they've done before."

"It doesn't seem to take much to piss them off, so that should be really easy."

Sean laughed but noticed Jill wasn't laughing.

"It doesn't seem to take much for them to feel insulted. We seem to have done it without even trying."

"I don't know if I can wait for two more dinners, Sean. How about I bring them something tomorrow and sit down to eat with them, like a coffee cake. Then when we go to the next dinner, we'll bring the something special just for them. Extra strong."

"Now you're thinking like a real master mind."

The evening passed quickly with both of them busy doing things around the cottage. Jill made a small coffee cake that she'd bring with her when she went up to get the list of errands the next morning.

They both slept soundly and the next morning Jill was anxious to put their plan in motion. For Sean it was a late night at his bookstore so he slept in. Jill went directly to the Charmeins carrying the coffee cake on a plate. She knocked on the door and Noah opened it almost immediately.

"What have we here? More dessert?"

"No, a coffee cake. And I would love to have a piece with a cup of coffee if you have a few minutes to enjoy it. I made it from scratch." Noah gave her the narrow eyes and then opened the door wide, allowing her entry. He handed her his list as she walked by.

"Bring it into the parlor and I'll make us some coffee. Charley will be down presently."

Jill sat in her usual seat in the parlor and waited for Noah to bring the coffee in. Several minutes later he came in carrying cups, saucers, and a coffee pot on a tray. A small refrigerator, which Jill had never noticed before, was snugged under the serving table. Noah took out cream from it which he poured into a small creamer.

"Do you take your coffee black, my dear?" He seemed genuinely polite.

"Well, I'm not a coffee drinker but I will have just half a cup with cream. Thank you." A sadness came over her when she thought about what kind of a relationship they might have had instead of the hateful, evil one she and Sean had endured with the Charmeins. She missed her parents and thought how her mother would have been around Charley's age if she was still alive. At that moment, Charley appeared at the other end of the parlor, making her way to her usual seat. Her coffee cup sat at her spot on the table. Jill quietly sipped her coffee, holding the cup in her hand. Noah then served them each a slice of the coffee cake on fine china plates.

"I hope you like it. It was my mother's recipe."

Charley looked a little odd to Jill and then she realized, once again, it was the missing champagne flute.

"And how is your mother? Do you see her often? Does she live in New York City?"

"My parents passed away - they were killed in the tsunami that took place in Indonesia. Over 200,000 people were killed by that tsunami. They were on vacation, well, sort of, but mostly volunteering through the Peace Corps. This was their first trip with the Peace Corps."

"Well, isn't that just dreadful. But then dying violently is always a dreadful way to die, don't you agree? Perhaps they should have restricted their volunteering to their own country." Jill was shocked that Charley laughed a little after she'd said this. She obviously saw some sick humor in it. Jill just ignored her or, God forbid, she might say something to insult Charley. So odd that they never saw anything they said as insulting to someone else. They were so bizarre, both Charley and Noah. And then she realized, they could never have been substitutes for her parents who were so loving and giving. She felt a tear forming in the corner of her eye and to quickly change the path her thinking was taking, she thought about the cruel landlords that she and Sean have lived with these past few months.

Charley held up her coffee cup, similar to her champagne flute, and Noah poured her a refill. She had taken the tiniest bite of the coffee cake and Noah finished the small piece he had cut for himself. Jill also ate her piece and sipped a little more of the coffee and then announced that it was time for her to leave.

"I have my own errands to do today, also. I'll be back later to drop yours off."

"Fine, and please do mention again to your husband about the leaves. They are continuing to pile up. I really don't want to have to keep asking." And Noah waved her away. Charley didn't seem to notice that Jill had stood up to leave the room and continued sipping her coffee which made Jill wonder if Noah had slipped a little champagne into Charley's cup.

Jill completed all her errands and while waiting for Sean to come home that night, she worked on a couple of art pieces. She was feeling so stressed with the plans they had for the Charmeins that she just couldn't get into painting anything serious. But she was feeling inspired, so she worked on an older painting that she had started a while back and was satisfied with the progress she was making. Time, as usual, passed quickly when she was painting and then she heard Sean coming in the front door.

"Hey, babe, how are you? You look tired tonight."

"Yeah, I am, pretty beat. Busy night but I just feel drained. I wish I had more time to write. Running the bookstore and trying to do anything else is just wearing me out. I didn't even take time to eat lunch."

"Which reminds me." Jill whispered, pointing to the ceiling, their sign for letting each other know the Charmeins were listening. She wrote on the pad of paper:

"Noah mentioned having you rake the leaves again. You should deal with him directly or he might make our lives more miserable if he thinks I'm not telling you."

Sean nodded his head wearily.

"What would you like for dinner?"

"What do we have?"

"How about something simple, like spaghetti and a jar of sauce."

"Sounds perfect."

"That works for me because I was painting and I didn't eat lunch, either. So, do you want a glass of wine?"

Jill poured a glass of wine for herself and one for Sean and set about cooking the pasta and heating the sauce.

Sean picked up the pad of paper and pencil and wrote a message to Jill. She leaned over his shoulder while he wrote:

"*How did the coffee cake work out - did they eat any?*" Jill nodded and gave him two thumbs up.

Sean nodded and mouthed the word 'great'.

A few minutes later they were sitting at the table silently eating. Jill felt her good mood waning and was a little annoyed, but she also understood why Sean would be depressed. She was just clearing the table when Sean's cell phone went off. He usually shut it off when he got home but he must have forgot. Jill grabbed it and handed it to him.

"Hello? Oh, hi Brenda, what's up? It what? I, but how, I just left there an hour ago. How did it..." Jill put the dishes in the sink and sat down at the table next to Sean. He had his head down with the phone pressed to his ear as if trying to listen more closely to the words that Brenda was saying to him.

"Alright, I'll be right there. No? But is anything salvageable? I mean, is everything..." Jill jumped up, uneasy over Sean's half of the conversation. She was sure they were talking about his bookstore. She couldn't imagine what might have happened. But she was beginning to piece together something based on what Sean was saying. She just wanted him to get off the phone so she could find out exactly what had happened, so she could hear him say the words.

"Why didn't they just call me? Oh, yeah right, ok. Well, thank you for that, Brenda. Sorry you had to be the one to get the call. Ok, I'll be there in the morning." He ended the call and, turning to Jill, started to cry. Jill had never seen him cry before, except when her parents were killed. That was the only time and that was a good reason to cry. But now she was scared and, wrapping her arms around his neck, he stood up and they held each other, crying together.

"Sean, please, what happened? The bookstore?"

"It's gone. Fire."

"Oh my God, oh my God!" And they cried together. They spent the night wrapped in each other's arms and fell asleep in bed that way.

The next morning Sean was up early and got ready to go to the store to assess the damage. Jill wanted to go with him, so she ran up to the mansion to pick up the errand list. She reached for the knocker and the door was, was usual, flung open.

"And here you are. We did enjoy your coffee cake. Here is your plate and here is the errand list." He was about to shut the door when he hesitated. Jill turned as she was about to sprint back to the cottage to go with Sean to the bookstore or at least see what was left of it.

"So sorry about your man's store. Books, wasn't it? And we look forward to him cleaning up our yard now. Tell him that, won't you?" Again, shock filled Jill's face as she digested the words Noah had just thrown at her. How? How, she wondered, could he know? This just happened. He had to have had something to do with it. There was no other way he could have known. And the door slammed in her face once again.

Chapter 13

She was shaking when she reached Sean's truck, which was running and waiting for her to get in. They drove off but Sean had to know what had upset her this time.

"Now what? Can't you ever go to their house without them pissing you off or saying something rude? What was it this time, babe? I don't know if I can deal with much more."

"He knew about the fire, Sean! How could he know about the fucking fire?" She was visibly shaking. Sean felt sick and gripped the steering wheel tighter. He felt his foot press down harder on the gas pedal and in a few minutes felt Jill's hand on his arm.

"Sean, please slow down, you're scaring me." He tried to calm down but all he could think about was how his landlords could possibly be involved in him losing his business. It just didn't make any sense to him. He had to know more. But to calm Jill down, he eased his foot off the gas pedal. He was just about ready to turn the truck around to confront the evil twins in the mansion but decided he needed to hear all the details.

"What exactly did he say, Jill, that would confirm for you that they were involved in the fire? Did he just admit it outright?" He tried to remain calm - he didn't want Jill to think he was upset or yelling at her in any way. His anger was reserved for the Charmeins only.

"He said, 'Sorry about your man's store.' They don't even remember our fucking names, Sean. We are nothing to them, just someone to do their errands and clean their huge mansion. How can people be so self-centered, lack so much compassion for anyone except themselves because, after all, I have insulted them and they got so upset by that. But they can make rude comments about my dead parents and that's ok. They can somehow reach out to whoever might be interested in selling my art in New York, and force them to change their minds. They can cause me to lose a job at the elementary school. And now, now, how can they possibly find someone who will set your bookstore on fire? But there it is, those are the facts."

Sean drove, barely seeing the road he was so focused on the words that Jill was saying. It was madness. It seemed impossible. It just could not be true but there was no other explanation.

"Did he say anything else?"

"No, I don't, no wait, he did. He said, 'we look forward to him raking our yard', or cleaning up our property, something like that. And, oh yeah, he wanted to be sure that I told you this. He wants you to know that it was him, or them. That they are responsible for you losing your business, Sean. Why can't we go to the police? There must be something they can do about this."

"Like what? No one was killed, not yet anyway. They would call it speculation, that's all. We have no proof that the Charmeins have been involved in any of this. What I want to know is why are they out to get us? What did we do to them? Is this just about wanting someone to do their house cleaning and garden work? It can't possibly be about that."

Jill was quiet as she thought about what Sean had just said.

"What did we do to them? Well, we tried to poison them and we are going to try to poison them again. Maybe, somehow, they know that."

"But we've never discussed anything about the poison in the house. We figured out we were being bugged before we ever talked about any of that."

"But still, maybe they know, somehow."

Before they knew it, they were at the bookstore, or what was left of it. They were happy to have arrived without being pulled over by a cop for driving way over the speed limit.

The building was cordoned off with yellow tape to keep people out. The building, although still standing, was scorched from fire. Most of the front of the building was made of wood and glass pane windows, which were gone. The frame work was metal and brick. They looked through what used to be the picture windows and saw books scattered everywhere, ruined mostly from water damage when the firefighters were trying to put the fire out. Many of the wooden bookshelves were completely destroyed. Sean felt a tear run down his cheek. Jill wrapped her arms around him and held him tight, hoping to squeeze the sadness out of him. While they stood there, Brenda came up to them and wrapped her arms around the both of them.

"Oh my God, Sean, I'm so sorry about this. This is just awful. I can't believe it."

"Hi, Brenda. Yup, it is."

"What are you going to do now?"

"Well, I'll do what I have to do to satisfy the insurance company. Maybe I'll rebuild. Or maybe this is a sign that I just need to finish my novel." He managed a small smile at Jill, who knew that wasn't possible since they'd have no income coming in now. She didn't have a lot in her savings from her parents, but she was still determined not to touch it. Sean would have to get a job.”

"Oh, I’m sorry Sean, I guess no one told you yet. The police filled out their report and when they called me last night, they said that a coffee pot had been left on and that was what started the fire. So, hopefully the insurance won’t consider it negligence. I’m sorry I didn’t mention it last night. The call was just so upsetting and I just wanted to let you know about the fire as soon as possible. I didn’t even think about the possibility of the insurance denying a claim or anything like that.”

Sean patted Brenda on the back, assuring her she didn’t have to worry about not telling him last night. He might not have slept at all if he had also known about this. Brenda left soon after, too upset about looking at the beautiful bookstore where she had worked for so many years, even before Sean had bought it. Sean and Jill went to a local coffee shop to talk.

Sean ordered a black coffee and Jill ordered a tea. They found an empty booth and sat. Neither of them was hungry. They were quiet for a while and then Jill spoke.

"How could you leave the building with the coffee pot on? That isn’t like you Sean, unless you were really tired.”

Sean was still stirring the little bit of sugar that he put in his coffee. He stopped and looked up at Jill.

"No, it doesn’t sound like me, does it. That’s because I didn’t, Jill. But I’m not going to be able to prove that. This was a setup. And I’m sure we both know who’s responsible.”

"But they never leave the house, which would mean that they hired someone. We should be able to find that out. We can get an investigator. Didn’t you have a hidden camera? We should see if someone came onto the property after you left."

"Yes, you're right. We should be able to find something, as long as it wasn't destroyed in the fire. I think my computer was destroyed. At least I brought my laptop home so I have some of the financials. And fortunately, I always copy a backup onto my laptop."

"But what difference does this make if the insurance claims negligence and denies your claim?"

"I don't know. I've never been in this situation before. I guess I have some research to do to find out what my options are if they think it was negligence. There has to be something. We need to go back to the store now and see what we can salvage. We'll have to take inventory. Maybe we can build in the same place, I'll buy metal shelving, not wood. But there has to be some books that are still ok that I can save. And I'll have a fire sale, you know, maybe some of the books are ok but smell a little smoky. Some people might not mind."

Jill sat quietly while Sean rambled, almost in a rant. She knew he had to do this. Most likely he was in shock. This is certainly how she was feeling, so she could only imagine the anxiety and stress he must be feeling.

Tears ran down her cheek and she tried to hide them from Sean. Their lives had just fallen apart, in the few months since they'd moved to the cottage. They were on top of the world then and now neither of them had a job or even a business. Everything they'd both worked so hard for had been taken away from them. She couldn't get an art show no matter where she called. Sean might not be able to get any insurance payout to rebuild. That meant he would want to use her money, the savings her parents had left her, to build a new bookstore. He loved the bookstore and his dream was to have book signings for his own books, to build clientele. Now he had nothing. He might not even have a client list anymore. She hoped he had backed everything up to his laptop like he said he did. And there went any dream of having a home or a child. She was already almost thirty and Sean was thirty-four. She didn't want to be an old parent. It seems all of their dreams went up in flames along with the bookstore. She didn't want to start over - she didn't have the energy.

They both sat in silence, each staring blankly into their cups. Sean reached over and took her hand and the tears began pouring down her face.

"We can do this. But I can't do it without you, babe."

Jill wiped the tears from her face. She knew she had to be strong, stay strong, for Sean. She couldn't throw anything else at him but she wondered how much was still owed on the property. There had to be something they could do. He couldn't possibly think about paying off the loan for the property, that was now a burnt-out shell, and then think about rebuilding on top of that. They would somehow have to get out of this mess, go in a different direction. They had to get an investigator and possibly a lawyer but they had no money. Sometimes there are lawyers who'd work pro bono if you have an interesting enough case. But she doubted any private investigators worked for free. Still, she did have her savings. They could use that money. And then all of their savings would be gone. They had to take one thing at a time.

"You know, I still owed money to the bank on the loan to buy the bookstore. I didn't even think about that. And now there is no bookstore. I think we need a lawyer."

"But how can we pay for them?"

"I know you don't want to but we'll have to use the savings." Sean put his head down, leaning on his elbow and covering his eyes with one hand, reaching out for Jill's hand with his other. The posture of defeat. Jill nearly burst out with tears. Instead, she swallowed the urge and held Sean's hand tightly.

Sean needed to get out of the coffee shop. He needed to walk back to the bookstore. He needed to see if there was anything salvageable. He jumped up suddenly, nearly overturning the small table. Jill grabbed the table to steady it.

"I've got to get out of here. Let's go back to the store and see if we can find the camera, something that shows I didn't leave the coffee pot on. And see if maybe someone broke in and set the fire. There has to be something."

They left the coffee shop and walked back to the bookstore. Inside they found the safe, covered in debris from the burnt walls and shelving but intact. Sean opened the safe and found everything as it was the night before. They walked outside and around to the back entrance where he had one camera set up but found nothing. The camera had been removed from the building.

"Do you have your phone? Take some photos. This is right where the camera was set up, pointed at the back door."

"I guess that will only count if you also took photos of the camera when it was there. The insurance company can say, well, how do we know there was a camera there just because you say there was. You need proof. How about a receipt for the cameras? Do you still have that?"

"Possibly, but buried down in the files in the basement. Those should be ok since the damage all seems to be up here. I bought those cameras when I bought the store back more than ten years ago now."

Back inside the store Jill walked around looking through the debris, wishing something would jump out at her and scream 'look at this - proof the fire had been deliberately set'. But she saw nothing. The coffee pot, which was glass, had exploded and pieces covered the floor around where the two-burner hot plate sat. Jill looked at the plug that was still in the wall and pulled it out. The cord near the plug looked like it had been scraped at, to expose the wires, possibly causing them to short out and start the fire. She knew then this had been planned and it was definitely a set up. She snapped photos of the plug and called Sean over to see it, too.

"I think I have something here. This plug was clearly tampered with as you can see. It didn't matter whether or not you had left the pot on, the cord would start a fire where it was plugged into the wall outlet."

Sean kissed her on the top of her head and taking her phone, took several more photos.

"I think we need to take this home with us, just in case someone comes back and tries to remove any evidence of this tampering."

Jill nodded agreement and they took the hot plate with its damaged plug out of the store and put it in his truck. They found some blue tarps that he had in a storage area and used them to cover where the windows had been, and then headed home.

♟ ♟

Your presence is requested at the home of
Noah and Charlotte Charmein.
The occasion: Dinner and drinks
Date: Sunday, December 15
Time: 6:30pm
Dinner will be served promptly at 7pm
after drinks and hors d'oeuvres in the parlor.
Dessert and coffee will follow dinner
after a short rest in the parlor.
We request that you arrive on time.

The monthly invitation was sitting in the box when they arrived home. Sean was tempted to rip it to shreds but Jill stopped him. She knew they had to go to this dinner. This was another chance to put an end to the Charmeins and get on with their lives, as the new owners of the Stirling Manor. There had to be money hidden somewhere in the house and they were determined to find it and share some of the wealth with the rightful descendent, Drew Stirling. Maybe they could buy the man a home to live in instead of living on the street and getting food from kind neighbors in town. They would make sure he was set up for the rest of his life. The first place she would check would be Charley's room. She never did get into that room. And she had a feeling it was ripe with secrets.

Sean walked over to the stereo and blasted some hard rock music.

"Sean, what are you doing? I can't hear myself think." Jill covered her ears to block the loud music.

"But, you can talk and I will hear you. I don't know why I didn't think of this before. This should blast their listening device, whatever they are using, but we can still talk."

"Clever, very clever. Ok, so what's the plan? I think we just need to go for it, make the best dessert that they can't refuse to eat and load it with whatever you bought to put into it. I don't want to know the details, I just want to know that it works."

"Yeah, it will work, don't worry about that. We just have to somehow get them to eat it. That is the tricky part."

"But what about Noah knowing that you lost the store. What about that? Are you going to confront them?"

"You know what, it will all be over soon. I'm not going to worry about any of that. We'll just let ah, nature, take its course. I have a new outlook on life, Jill, and we are finally going to come out on top. Within the week we are going to be living in that mansion. All of our worries will be over. Bookstore, what bookstore? You'll be painting, inspired by some of the most beautiful paintings in the world hanging on the walls at Stirling Manor. And I'm going to sit down and write my novel, wherever and whenever I want. We are going to find Drew Stirling and, after we find the money, give a fair share of it to Drew, or maybe set up a bank account for him. Life will be grand!"

"What are we going to do with the bodies?" Jill was being practical but Sean had not thought that far ahead.

"Oh, yes, the bodies. Whatever will we do with the bodies? Freezer?"

Jill shook her head.

"Chop them up and throw them in the meat grinder?"

Jill made a gesture as if puking.

"Bury them in the back yard or put them in the furnace. I haven't been in the basement, but it must have a huge furnace to service the entire mansion."

"Ok, I like either of those options better." Jill really was feeling nauseous and stopped to let herself think about what they were actually discussing: killing both of their landlords. She could never picture herself in this position and even now she wouldn't allow herself to think seriously about it. It was ok to joke with Sean as if he was writing a scene in a novel, but to think about performing any of these acts on real people, even though they were the worst, most evil people she had ever encountered in her life, gave her a deep-rooted sick feeling in her gut. She didn't want to talk about them anymore and changed the subject.

"So, what kind of dessert are we going to make?"

"How about 'forearm banana bread' or maybe 'sweet bread pudding with blood raspberry sauce' or a nice slice of 'buttock pie'?" Sean was not ready to let it go.

"Ok, Sean, can we stop now? I can't think about this anymore." He saw the paleness in Jill's face. He noticed that she had put her hand to her mouth to stop whatever might come up. Changing the subject was a good idea.

"Sorry babe. I just had to think about something else to forget everything that has happened to us in the few short months that we've lived here. And, I'm sure of it now, they've been behind all of it. They did this to us. So, yeah, sweet revenge. I have no feelings for these people at all. How could I? Do you?"

"No, but it is so dreadful that we are resorting to this."

"Think about it. They have no relatives, who will miss them?"

"Well, we don't really have any relatives either. Who would miss us?"

Chapter 14

Sean hated to admit it but it was true. After Jill's parents had died, her brother just disappeared. And Sean never had a close relationship with either of his siblings. His dad left the family when he was about ten years old. His mom remarried and moved to some island, he couldn't remember which one. He heard several years ago that his brother, a lifetime soldier, was killed overseas, but he wasn't sure. His sister became a nun but she never got in touch with him to tell him this, so he wasn't even sure if that was true. So, neither he nor Jill had any relatives who would miss them. They were actually more like the Charmeins than they realized. Although they were nowhere near as insensitive and, as Jill called them, evil. He would never treat people the way the Charmeins had treated he and Jill.

They ate their dinner in silence again that night. They turned the loud music off since neither of them had any more energy to talk. They both felt like they had so much to do, particularly concerning the bookstore. But they also felt like they just didn't know where to start. Jill was mostly pushing her food around on her plate. She knew they had to have a plan. Instead of turning the music back on, which was giving her a headache, she spoke in a whisper.

"We have to just start writing down a list of what we need to do concerning the bookstore and the fire that was obviously set by our landlords. And yes, I know, we can't prove that but we know it is true, so we will proceed as if this will also be known by the insurance company and the police, if we need to involve them. Which I think we do. So, we'll sit down tomorrow and start writing a list, ok. That will give us some focus. And then we can bake the cake and prepare to meet with them, hopefully for the last time." When she said 'them' she pointed towards the mansion. Sean, of course, knew who she meant.

But Sean could barely hear her, particularly when she started talking about the Charmeins. He raised up out of his seat so she could whisper directly into his ear. When she finished what she had to say, he got up and took the pad of paper and pencil from the living room coffee table and brought it over to the dinner table and wrote:

"I think our problems will all be solved when we have our final meeting with the Charmeins. Once we meet them and give them dessert, which they will not be able to resist, we should be able to sleep knowing that by morning they will be gone once and for all. So instead of writing a list, why don't we just focus on making that fabulous dessert and getting rid of the bodies. That is the only plan we need to work on." He slid the pad of paper and pencil over to Jill who started writing furiously:

"We keep talking about 'dessert'. But, I think we are looking at the wrong menu item. We don't know if they ever ate anything we brought, except the coffee cake that I also ate because it wasn't poisoned. But I don't think we can miss if instead we bring some champagne that is tainted. Can you get some of the poison into a bottle with a hypodermic needle?"

Sean loved that idea and kissed the top of Jill's head. He took the pad and pencil back and responded:

"Or, we can do both. But I was thinking, how do we prevent Noah from pouring some of the champagne into our glasses?"

Jill replied: *"Well, they usually don't open what we bring them so perhaps they will drink it when we aren't there. And we'll know they are gone if Noah doesn't come to the door in the morning.*

But I do like the idea of the champagne and the cake - we can't miss with both of them tainted."

Sean nodded agreement. He was more excited about this plan than thinking about anything to do with his bookstore. That just made him feel exhausted, defeated, and hopeless. He didn't think of himself as a person who sought revenge, but with the Charmeins, a different person inhabited his soul, one he hoped to never meet again. It was true, people can bring out the worst in you or the best in you. He thought of a play on words for a quote he'd heard many years ago, "The best in you brings out the worst in me." Or maybe an old girlfriend once said that to him. But thinking about the Charmeins, he thought "The beast in you brings out the worst in me." Maybe he'd made up the whole 'best in you brings out worst in me' but it did seem that some people could do that. He liked his interpretation though, since the Charmeins were like evil beasts. And they certainly have brought out the worst in him and Jill, too, which he never thought he would see. But this is the change that can happen in you when you meet such evil. He and Jill were actually planning their deaths. And he felt so unattached to following through with this deed, it's like he had no feelings, no sympathy, for the two people who would be their victims. He just wanted it to be over with.

He reached across the table to Jill who seemed to be lost in her own thoughts. They both sat, holding hands at the table, and didn't speak.

They cleaned up the dinner dishes, in silence, and sat on the couch, each with a glass of wine and the pad of paper and pencil.

"So, will you buy the champagne tomorrow - did you happen to notice what kind they drink?" Jill was good at planning and wanted to get all the details worked out.

"Yes, a nice champagne, an expensive one. It's quite a bit more than the champagne we usually have. I think that's what we brought them. They kind of acted like we'd brought them a bottle of cooking wine. I don't think they'll turn their noses up at their own preference. I have to go to the bookstore tomorrow so I'll pick up the champagne on my way home."

"Ok, good."

"What are you going to do at the store? Do you want me to go with you?"

"No, I'm going to get in there and get dirty, start seeing what I can salvage. Also try to board it up better so it isn't just using the tarps as protection."

"But if our plan works then you won't need to do anything with the bookstore. You can have it all leveled."

"I can't throw any books out if they are salvageable. Even if I can get half-price for them. Yes, I know we have 'the plan' but I still have respect for all the books that are alive and well, so to speak."

'Brenda sent me a text and said if I want to go there to let her know and she would help me with whatever I needed help with."

"She's a good lady."

"Yes, she is."

"Did you hear from Jennie?"

"Brenda talked to her - she has enough of her own problems at home. She'll get another job somewhere."

Both exhausted, they decided to go to bed early. Sean had to get up early and go to the bookstore to see what he could find that wasn't burnt to a crisp. He also needed to buy some wood panels to board up the front of the store. He could tell there wasn't a lot that could be saved but what there was, he wanted to take it out of the store and bring it home. He could fit a lot in the back of his truck, so first he would stop at a grocery store to pick up some boxes for the books. He knew he wouldn't be able to make much of a dent in just a day, but he had to start some time, just start somewhere. He was hoping he was wrong and that there was more that he could save than what he'd seen in their initial assessment of the damages.

♟ ♟

Sean had set the alarm for 6am. He was up and out of the house before Jill got up. He didn't want to disturb her - he knew they were both exhausted from the day before and since he didn't sleep that well, there was no sense in both of them not having a good night's sleep.

Jill woke feeling like she'd had only a couple of hours of sleep even though she'd had a solid eight hours. She knew Sean wanted to leave early, but was disappointed that she didn't get to give him a hug before he'd left. More than ever they both needed each other's support. She stretched out on the bed, tempted to curl back up and pull the covers over her head. But she had to get up. And then she remembered. This was the day, this was it. They were ending this torture that they've dealt with for these past four months. Had it really only been just four months? She couldn't believe how their lives had been turned upside down in such a short span of time.

She got up and showered. She wasn't hungry, but made herself a bowl of hot oatmeal and a cup of herbal tea. She sat in the living room, eating without really tasting the oatmeal even though she'd cut up banana and added cinnamon, honey, and soy milk. She felt like she couldn't think anymore. She felt like she was waiting, waiting for the hour, the minute, when they would go to the Charmeins one last time, have one last meal with them, give them the champagne and the cake, and leave to go home, knowing that in the morning they would be gone. Forever. She shivered thinking about what they would face in the morning. No cops, no ambulance. They wouldn't call anyone. No one knew who they were and no one would know they were gone. She couldn't help but feel a little sad about the situation, but the Charmeins had chosen this outcome. They chose to destroy the lives of her and Sean. And she never felt so helpless in her life.

She just couldn't understand why they would do this - just to have someone to clean their mansion and maintain their grounds? They must have so much money they could hire someone, and they did have paid help before she and Sean had arrived. But was it just them? She couldn't help but think they very possibly had done this before. She and Sean couldn't have been the first to act as pawns in their game. Their game, that was it. It was a game for them. They didn't care about her or Sean or what they might want to do with their lives. It was all a game of control. Control and destroy. Well, they were going to get a taste of their own medicine now. Why should the Charmeins have all this wealth and live in this beautiful mansion while she and Sean struggled to make ends meet, only to have everything they've worked so hard for, everything they've ever wanted in their lives, to eventually have a small home and a baby, everything just taken away from them. All their dreams shattered.

She felt tears welling up in her eyes and put her oatmeal down on the coffee table. She let herself go, crying from the pit of her stomach, from the place in her heart that holds everything of any worth to her, that makes her life worth living. She felt it all crumbling into tiny pieces and coming out through the tears she shed. She was sobbing now, loudly and more deeply than she'd ever thought possible. Only one other time had she felt such a deep sadness, longing for something that meant more to her than her own life. That was when she'd heard her parents had died. She'd remember that day for as long as she lived and how in those few seconds when the phone rang and she talked to someone she didn't know who'd informed her that her parents had been killed in a tsunami, a tsunami for Christ's sake, how in that moment she knew her life had been changed forever. The life force drained from her at that moment. If she didn't have Sean in her life she may have ended her own.

She sipped at her tea and walked into the bathroom to wash her face. She knew crying didn't help any situation but she knew she usually felt better when she let everything go and got the sadness out of her. She didn't realize the depth of pain she was feeling and how many memories were coming up. Sometimes you just swallow the sadness because you can't fall apart; you have to work at your job and make money to pay the rent and do your laundry and food shopping and vacuuming. You have to get up every day and make your bed and shower. You can't pull the covers over your head and hide from all the sadness that lives in your gut and in your heart. You just have to swallow it all. And then, at a moment like this, it all surfaces, it all comes up reminding you that you are human and emotions run very deep. You aren't always happy and smiling. You may feel a sadness unlike anything you've ever felt before, but you go on living. You have to go on living. She always believed the easy way out was taking your own life. It is so much harder going on with your sadness, living with your pain every day. That made her stronger, eventually. But the pain was always there, would always be there. She knew that at any minute she could fall apart. But she had to be strong, she had to live her life and whatever came with it. She would never give up. For herself, for Sean, for her parents.

She jumped in the shower and let all the sadness wash out of her and down the drain. For now.

She walked up to the mansion and, using the lion-head knocker, knocked forcefully on the door. Noah opened it quickly.

"I'm here, I'm here. And here is your list. Please bring everything from the list back as soon as possible. And please be prompt tonight." She didn't even get a word out and the door slammed shut.

Jill went to the store and got everything on his list and then bought the items she needed for their dessert. She couldn't wait for the evening and hoped Sean didn't come home too tired. She knew he wanted to do as much as he could at the bookstore, salvaging as many books as he could. But she wanted to get everything right. She hoped he remembered to pick up the champagne. They didn't have quality champagne in their local supermarket - they didn't carry anything that expensive, just had the usual inexpensive champagnes. She decided to text Sean to remind him.

"Hi, how's the store clean-up going?" She waited a few minutes while sitting in her car at the supermarket. He finally texted back.

"Good, I've got about four boxes of good undamaged books so far. And there are quite a few that I could sell half-price so it's not a total loss. How are you?"

"Ok, I'm at the supermarket - don't forget to pick up the champagne, ok?"

"Already did - I got boxes at the supermarket here in Lebron - they have a ton. I talked to the manager, told him my situation. He was sympathetic and had heard about it - his wife buys her books from us. He'll save boxes for me, whatever I need."

"Great. I'm heading home. Going to work on that cake."

"Wait till I get home - I'll be home early this afternoon."

"Please don't be late. We need to prepare for tonight." Jill was very careful about how she worded her texts because she knew people could look at texts and they could count as evidence in murder trials.

"Yes, I promise. Brenda and I had a bite to eat and we'll be done in just a few more hours. I'll call when I'm on my way home."

Jill delivered the items from the list to the Charmeins, without a word exchanged, not even a thank you from Noah, and went home to get everything she and Sean would need to make the cake that night. She was exhausted from the morning and all the memories that had resurfaced after so many years. She lay down for a nap and waited for Sean's call.

Suddenly, she jumped awake when she heard a vehicle outside. The cottage was dark so she put a few lights on. It did get dark earlier now since it was almost winter, but she had expected Sean to be home by now. She looked out the window and saw his truck pulling into the yard.

Chapter 15

Sean came into the house looking exhausted. But he was pumped and went straight into the kitchen to start working on the cake. Jill followed behind him.

"Hey, I thought you were going to be home earlier?"

"Hey babe." Sean turned and gave Jill a big hug then started preparing the cake pans.

"Yeah, sorry, you know how it is when you're on a roll. I just needed to get some more work done. And I did. I have ten boxes of books in great shape that I can charge full-price for. I also filled a couple of boxes with ones that'll sell for half price. And there are lots more. Some bookshelves hadn't been touched at all. The fire started in the office so my desk, as you saw, is gone and some of the shelving in that area. Of course, everything made of wood in the office area was damaged. But, thankfully, there are more books that are salvageable than we originally thought. So, let's get this cake ready. We can get this on and then I'll take a shower and then we'll go to the Charmeins. Here's the champagne, too, nice and chilled."

Jill put her fingers to her lips and pointed to the ceiling. Sean nodded. He found the pad of paper and pencil and wrote:

"Thanks for the reminder. I was just about to say, 'What a shame to ruin a nice bottle of champagne with poison.'"

"Why don't I whip up the cake while you shower. The oven is heating up and I just have to get dressed." She spoke in a soft whisper. She was so tired of having to screen everything they said to each other. Or write it down, making sure they destroyed the slips of paper afterwards. The thought of getting their privacy back inspired her and she made a mixed berry filling for the cake. When Sean had showered and dressed, they finished the cake together, icing it when it had cooled. It was about 5:45pm by the time everything was ready. He just had to prepare the champagne.

"Ok, last chance. Do we keep it for ourselves or prepare it special for the neighbors." Jill could tell he was tired because his scribbled message was barely legible.

"We want to be sure. Do it. We'll buy another bottle when we are in the mansion."

"Good point."

"You know, they might not eat the cake but we can almost guarantee that they'll drink the champagne."

"So true. Ok, let me get it ready. Just remember not to drink too much tonight."

"Absolutely. I'm going to stick to water mostly. You know Noah is always right there with the champagne. I'll have to keep my glass covered. That goes for you, too."

"Of course. Water mostly. And maybe just half a glass from the bottle of champagne that Charley will already have open, but nothing with dinner. I'll tell them how tired I am - no thanks to them and their hands in burning down my bookstore."

"I can't believe how composed you are when you are about to meet the enemy. We know he did this or paid someone to do it. I would want to scratch his eyes out."

"We're almost out of this. I'm not going to lose it now."

Sean finished preparing the champagne, they got the cake, and walked up to the mansion. The big, intimidating, overpowering, almost sinister hulking estate, Stirling Manor would soon be their home to enjoy. Jill used the lion-head knocker for what she hoped would be the last time. Never would she ever have to do any more errands for the ungrateful, evil twosome. She couldn't help but smile and nearly started laughing when Noah swung open the door.

"Oh, yes, it is that time again, isn't it. Follow me." And he turned and walked towards the parlor with Sean and Jill following.

"Look my dear, they brought us gifts. Another cake. Good heavens. Oh, and something you might like my dear. Your favorite champagne. Finally, they brought something we actually like."

Charley lay in her chaise lounge, champagne glass held high as if in the middle of a toast.

"Oh, well, fine dear. Put it in the other room please. With the other thing you have."

"A cake, is it? I believe it is another cake." Noah gave them both a smirk.

"Yes," Jill volunteered. "It is a cake. But a special recipe. With a mixed berry filling. I hope you like it."

Neither of them commented about the cake. Jill and Sean obediently took their usual seats. Noah sat in the chair closest to Charley.

As usual, Charley looked like she was already half in the bag. It always surprised Sean and Jill when she actually asked a serious question. She didn't look like she was coherent enough to think of anything serious to say.

"So, do tell us about the fire. I heard it was dreadful."

Jill couldn't believe she used the same word 'dreadful' when speaking about losing her parents. As if they were on an even par.

Sean spoke up when he saw the look on Jill's face. He wanted to keep the conversation as light and fluffy as possible so as not to give them any reason to suspect their behavior was anything but trustworthy.

"Well, yes, apparently it was a faulty plug that started the fire. So, I have a lot of paperwork to fill out to see what I can get from the insurance. And I've been gathering some of the books that weren't damaged. Then I'll look at rebuilding."

Jill gave Sean a look and he took her hand in his and squeezed it. He wanted her to just go with what he was saying. They hadn't talked about this, but Sean was looking for a confession and he thought he might get it if he just played dumb.

Noah and Charley exchanged glances.

"Oh, really? Hmm, so you might rebuild. Wasn't that negligence if the fire was caused by a faulty plug? Isn't that something you should have noticed?" Noah was trying his best to act only mildly interested.

"Well, if it was tampered with then it possibly was deliberately set and I'm not at fault. I'm having all this looked at, though - we have an investigator so we'll find out what really happened. Also, I had security cameras. So, if someone broke in, we should find that out, too."

Noah had a worried look on his face and, again, he and Charley exchanged the same, furtive glances. Charley always left these kinds of questions up to Noah and she distracted herself by watching the bubbles in her champagne glass.

"I was so hoping we could come to an agreement and you could now tend to our gardens. We do have a bit of land and need it taken care of. This, of course, would be in exchange for your rent."

"This is my business, Noah, the bookstore and writing. Both are very important to me, just as painting is very important to Jill."

"Oh, you young people do worry about the silliest things. Writing, painting, none of it means anything. No one really cares, you know. But a man's house is his castle. This is my castle. This is important, keeping it clean and well-manicured, inside and out."

"But it is your castle, Noah, not mine. Why should I care about your castle?"

"Because, my good man, there are the haves and the have-nots. We are the haves, you are the have-nots. Don't you see this? The book store is meaningless, as well. You are a slave to the economy. Accept your fate. Do as we wish. All will be good."

Sean and Jill stared at him, this crazy man, speaking his crazy words, living in his own crazy world, was throwing nonsense words at them. Sean was still hoping to bring the conversation back to the fire, still hoping to get a confession. But Noah was distracted now. He got up and poured more champagne into Charley's glass, who had been holding her flute up for several minutes. She relaxed when she saw the bubbles appear again. He came over to Jill to fill her glass but she covered it and shook her head. Sean, also, refused to accept any more champagne.

"Well, no more drinks. Must be time for dinner." He and Charley headed to the dining room. Jill and Sean followed, Jill clutching Sean's arm as tight as she could. He patted her hand reassuringly.

Again, the plate warmers were set up and roast beef, mashed potatoes, and sliced beets were on their plates. Dinner rolls were covered in a basket. Everything, again, arranged perfectly on the table. Jill and Sean took their usual seats at the table.

They ate in silence for several minutes.

"Does anyone want any more champagne? Or wine perhaps, to go with the meal? Seems a shame to not have a complimentary wine with this fabulous dinner we made just for you two."

Noah often resorted to guilt, as if he and Charley were going out of their way to prepare this wonderful meal just for Sean and Jill. Sean knew they didn't have anything else to do since he and Jill were taking care of all the cleaning and their errands. But Sean still wanted to find out more about the fire. He knew Noah had more information but was acting innocent, like he knew nothing about it.

Sean and Jill both shook their heads. After their last visit, Jill definitely was not going to drink to excess - she never wanted to feel as bad as she had then. Noah ignored their refusals and opened the wine anyway, pouring a glass for each of them.

"I insist." He and Charley picked up their glasses and turned to Jill and Sean to toast. Sean and Jill exchanged glances and obediently picked up their glasses and clinking all around, each took a tiny sip.

"Bon Appetit!" Noah took a gulp and he and Charley smiled at each other, burst out laughing, and then smiled at Sean and Jill. Sean and Jill looked at each other with faces that did not need any explanation, both apparently were thinking the same thing about their unstable and insane landlords.

Sean was trying to figure out how to approach the subject of the fire again without the Charmeins feeling insulted and throwing him and Jill out. He didn't want to give them any reason to throw out their cake or, God forbid, the expensive champagne he'd bought, particularly now that he didn't have any money coming in. Although he didn't make a lot at the bookstore, he'd always been able to give himself some semblance of a weekly pay check. He was pondering his pathetic situation when Noah spoke up.

"So, good news! We are no longer charging you rent for the cottage. Since you both work for us now, you can live there rent-free. Isn't that wonderful and most generous of us?"

"Oh yes, my dear, so generous. Too generous I would say." Charley couldn't say anything without taking a sip of alcohol. She loved her champagne so much Sean was surprised to see her drinking the red wine.

Noah waited for Sean and Jill to show their great appreciation in some way. When neither of them said anything but instead kept eating, Noah continued.

"Oh course, we'll have to explain, Sean, what we will need you to do for us. On the property, that is. There is a lot of work that should keep you busy through the seasons. I have a list I give all my gardeners, but we can talk about that when you come by tomorrow morning, with your wife. And we may need to beef up your work schedule a little, too, my dear. Seems you've been slacking somewhat. We found dust in one of the bedrooms, on the nightstand. We really need you to be more observant. We won't tolerate sloppy work. We just won't. Particularly since we aren't charging you to live in the cottage anymore. We demand perfection."

Charley listened to his speech, nodding agreement, raising her glass, she was back to champagne again, in acknowledgement to what Noah was saying.

Jill nearly choked on her roast beef. She knew that in some of the rooms, which were barely dusty, mostly from non-use the way dust seems to come from nowhere to cover everything whether or not the room is used, she would let them go and not bother wiping down the few dots of dust that she saw. But she realized that the Charmeins, or at least Noah, since Charley seemed unconcerned about everything except keeping the champagne flowing, went through the rooms and gave them the white glove test to see if Jill had actually dusted them.

"But no more talk about this tonight. Let's enjoy our meal and so many desserts. Here, let me top off your wine glasses." Noah, for some reason, was in a most agreeable mood. And Charley was Charley. There didn't seem to be much going on with her. Jill figured that by now, she was an alcoholic and that seemed to be the way Noah liked her. Jill still wondered about the medicine - she was never able to get into Charley's room but she was still convinced that it held many secrets. She was sure Charley must have some kind of cancer. Perhaps that was why she drank all the time. Perhaps she couldn't deal with either the pain or the dire prognosis. She wondered when Charley would have been to any doctors since they never left the mansion. But she must have at some time because she had a prescription that Jill picked up at the pharmacy. Maybe it wasn't anything serious after all. Maybe they were setting Sean and Jill up all along, making them believe Charley was ill when she wasn't. So many questions; Jill wished she had the answers.

Noah moved towards Jill's glass.

"No, no more for me, thank you." Noah nodded to Sean but he also covered his glass.

"So, we move to the parlor for coffee and dessert. Shall we, my dear." Noah put his arm out for Charley and led her to the parlor.

Sean and Jill exchanged looks as they followed the couple. Sean shook his head indicating that they were not going to stay for dessert. The plan was to leave the champagne and the dessert for the Charmeins. Sean didn't want to be in an awkward position of having to make excuses for not wanting to eat the dessert with them. He was sure Charley would be ok with not sharing her champagne. He was counting on it.

"Are you going to stay for coffee and dessert or are you going to run off again? I suppose one of these days we'll share a dessert. But if you must leave, we insist that you take a large slice of the wonderful seven-layer cake we made for you."

"Yes, we insist." Charley echoed.

"Well, I am quite tired. You know I spent the day at my bookstore. There were many books I was able to salvage that I can still sell because they are undamaged and I can put any that are slightly damaged in a half-price bin to get something for them. But I'm surprised that not as many books were damaged as I had originally thought. Since the fire started in my office, it took a little while for the fire to make its way to the books. Luckily a neighbor saw the fire and called the fire department immediately. So, if someone did set the fire, deliberately, they didn't plan on the wonderful neighbors we have who look out for each other." Sean waited for a response. He hoped this time to get Noah to admit something, or admit something that only someone who was responsible for the crime would know.

"Yes, negligence, that's what it sounds like to me. You were responsible. And the insurance companies don't pay when it is your fault. So, we'll see you in the morning."

"As I've already said, Noah, I'm going to my bookstore in the morning. I have a lot more cleaning up to do. I may stop by here later in the afternoon, if I get a chance."

"Well, I am disappointed. I thought for sure... Well, we'll see you, um, later." And he started laughing. Charley, it seemed without knowing why, joined in the laughter.

"Let me get you your cake now. Your coats are in the front closet. You can get them on your way out." Jill and Sean walked out of the parlor without saying good-bye to Charley, who didn't seem to notice that they were leaving anyway. They put their coats on and waited for Noah on the front step. Noah came down the hall carrying a plate with a large slice of the seven-layer cake on it, covered with plastic wrap. In his other hand he was carrying what looked like the bottle of champagne that they'd brought.

"Thank you." Jill was about to say that the champagne was for them when Noah handed them the plate and turned to go back to the parlor closing the door firmly behind him.

"You know, sometimes he seems almost nice and then other times just plain rude."

"No, he's just plain rude. I don't think he has a 'nice'." They stood there looking at the door with the lion knocker and then, turning to each other and smiling like a couple of school kids who've just played a prank, ran down to the cottage giggling all the way.

Chapter 16

Back at the cottage Jill and Sean were ecstatic. They were sure everything would work out this time, and the key ingredient had been champagne. Jill didn't know why they hadn't thought of this before. Especially since every time they visited the Charmeins they served champagne, and not just any champagne but the same expensive label. She wouldn't be surprised if they'd just thrown out the bottles she and Sean had brought to their previous dinners. Before they knew of Charley's personal preference for champagne, and one label in particular, they'd brought an inexpensive bottle of wine. No doubt that was dumped out. But this time, Charley's eyes lit up when she saw the familiar bottle they'd brought. This was a brilliant plan. Jill got two glasses and, although surely not as good as Charley's champagne, a bottle of wine to celebrate what was sure to be their victory.

Sean was relaxing on the sofa, leaning back, with paper and pencil in his hand. Jill brought the bottle and two glasses over and poured them each a full glass of wine. Then she went into the kitchen and got two small plates, two forks and cut them each a slice of the seven-layer cake. It looked and smelled delicious, chocolate with a raspberry filling. She cut herself a smaller piece because she was concerned about eating chocolate at night; it often kept her awake. By the time they got settled, it was almost 9:30 but she knew they probably wouldn't get much sleep. They would both be too excited thinking about going up to the mansion in the morning to see what had transpired and needed to set about planning how to get rid of the bodies. She sat next to Sean and they both took a bite of the cake. Jill closed her eyes in ecstasy - she loved a delicious piece of cake and one that was made with such tasty ingredients. She took the pad, inspired to write about the food they enjoyed each month at the Charmeins. She realized that this would be the last time she would have to write with pad and pencil since they would soon be living in the mansion themselves.

"Too bad we just killed our neighbors - they really were good cooks. This cake is heavenly."

Sean was scraping his plate clean and put it down to write:

"Yes, I agree. I guess this is what they did with their time. They learned how to be good cooks. Who knows, they may have done this in a life before they decided to take over Stirling Manor."

"It's too bad we never really learned anything about them. But they didn't seem to ever want to share anything. And they were only interested in us when it served their needs."

"True. But it was meant to be. Their legacy is over - there's a new sheriff in town." And Sean tipped his imaginary hat.

"I don't think I'll sleep a wink tonight - I'm too wound up. But just in case it didn't work, I will go up there at my usual time, around 8am."

Jill was feeling a little paranoid. The saying 'don't count your chickens before they are hatched', popped into her head. She wasn't going to really celebrate until she knew for sure, until she actually saw the two dead bodies.

"What do you mean 'in case it didn't work' - of course it worked. I put enough of my special potion in there to kill a horse!"

"Ok, I believe you. And you did see Noah carrying the bottle when we left, right?"

"Noah had it in his other hand and was heading to the parlor with it. I'm sure it is half-gone by now."

Jill felt uneasy about something and then she remembered what she wanted to ask. She took the pad and pencil:

"So, how do we get into the house?" Sean nodded and taking the pad and pencil and letting out a big sigh, began to write:

"Good question. When I raked that day, there were many keys in the garage hanging on a peg board. Noah doesn't know this, but I took some of the keys and tried several of them on the front door. I knew he thought I was raking so wouldn't be looking to see what I was doing. I found one that opened the front door. I guessed they would have had duplicates made at one time. They may have given one to the cleaning woman they had. There were also duplicates to the garage. I'm sure the gardener needed a key. I don't know if the Charmeins are aware of the duplicates though. They may have been more open, friendly, and trusting at one time. Who knows? When I went to get the key for the garage, he had it in the house."

"Interesting. So, good, there shouldn't be a problem getting into the house. Ok. Well, I don't know about you, but I'm really tired. This has been an exhausting day."

"I agree. And I have more to do at the bookstore tomorrow. I want to take as many books as I can out of there."

"Where will you store them?"

"Are you kidding? We have an enormous garage now. Remember I told you about it? Oh yeah, and we have a Mercedes and a Rolls Royce. Living in style, babe!"

Jill smiled and suppressed a yawn.

Jill went through her usual routine in the bathroom – which included burning their notes and flushing the ashes down the toilet – and when she went into the bedroom Sean was just climbing into bed. He walked over to her side of the bed and holding her close, whispered in her ear.

"How about we celebrate early?" He kissed her on the lips and down her neck. They fell onto the bed and made love as if it was for the last time.

Chapter 17

The ambulance pulled up to the front entrance and parked. Two EMTs got out. They took one emergency stretcher out of the back of the ambulance and when they brought it up the stairs, the front door opened and a cop greeted them.

"The bodies are in the bedroom. First door on the left."

The cop, officer Johnston, stood looking up at the mansion. A second cop, a rookie, officer Blake came out and stood next to Johnston, pulled his collar up around his ears, and put his hands in his pockets.

"It's a chilly one today, supposed to be getting a foot of snow. Will be nice for Christmas. The kids love the snow." Johnston rubbed his hands together, blowing warm air into them.

"Yeah, mine, too. So, what do you think? Double suicide?"

"I would say so. Has all the markings. Might have swallowed pills, whatever, and then lay down on the bed. Too bad. The guy might have been drunk, too; it appears he choked on his own vomit. Maybe they both took a ton of pills. Makes you wonder what kind of misery sends them over the edge like this. Must have had something really tragic happen in their lives. Maybe one of them had cancer or was really sick. You just don't know. No suicide note though; that would have helped us."

"Any family?" Officer Blake glanced up at the mansion where Johnston kept staring.

"I'll check it out when we get back to the station. What were their names, again?"

Officer Blake took out a notebook and checked his notes. "Sean and Jill Porter. That's all I've got so far. I'll look through the cottage and see if I can find out anything more."

The two EMTs came out with the first body. They put it in the back of the ambulance and brought the other emergency stretcher into the cottage.

"Who called it in? The people who live in that mansion?"

"No, a woman. Name's Brenda, Brenda Silven." Johnston flipped through the dispatch notes, double-checking the information he had.

"I guess this woman worked for the guy and he was supposed to show up at the bookstore. Get this, there was a fire at the bookstore and he nearly lost everything. It was his store and this Brenda was helping him salvage whatever they could from the fire. Sometimes these kinds of tragedies just tear a person apart and they never recover. Anyway, he was supposed to show up at the store two days ago and he never did and she couldn't get him on his phone so she was worried something had happened to him and his wife." Johnston turned his attention back to the mansion.

"Do we know anything about that mansion? It sure is huge."

"I don't know, I figure it's empty. I didn't even know it was there until we drove around the corner. It sure is hidden down in these woods. You'd never guess something that massive was built this far out in the middle of nowhere."

"This is pretty remote. They're kind of off the grid. Surprised they even have electricity or other services here. Must have personal generators for both." Officer Johnston walked down the steps and took a few more steps toward the mansion. The cottage door opened and the EMTs came out with the second body on the stretcher, put it in the back of the ambulance, and shut the door.

"Do you need anything else from us?"

"No, you're good to go."

"Great, if you want to know anything about the bodies, they should have the results of the autopsies in a week or so. Just call the hospital and they'll give you all the information, if you need it." The tall, thin EMT slouched, waiting for the officers to give him the ok.

"That's great, thank you boys." The EMTs got in the ambulance and drove away.

"Hey Blake, do you remember something like this happening a few years back, maybe five or six years, maybe less. I wasn't here then. But this sounds familiar to me." Johnston continued staring up at the mansion.

"No, I don't know. I wasn't even a cop then, sir. But I'll check it out, see what I can find. There must be some family around, or someone in town who would know if something like this has happened before."

Johnston wasn't satisfied that the place was empty and decided he needed to do a little more investigating. He'd talk with his Sargeant about his suspicions when he got back to the station.

They went back into the cottage for one more look around. The detectives would be here the next day to give the place a thorough inspection. But Johnston was hoping something might jump out at him, any clue that could provide a rational explanation for their apparent suicides.

"Hey, cake." Officer Blake saw the remains of what looked like a seven-layer cake with a reddish filling between the layers, maybe raspberry, or some kind of berry. He picked up the thin slice that was left on the plate and was ready to toss it into his mouth when officer Johnston grabbed his arm to stop him.

"What are you doing, rookie? This is evidence. Everything in this place is evidence. You don't just start eating any food that you see lying around. It could be poisoned. We have to bring it back to the lab, because, why Blake?"

"Because it's evidence. Yes sir, I got it."

"Thank you. There are a couple of plastic bags in the evidence collection kit. Take one out and put the cake in it. And in the future, you never eat anything in any home where suspicious deaths have happened. Do you understand? Particularly when you don't know how the victims have died. Tomorrow when the detectives are here, they'll check for gas leaks, pill bottles, any liquids they may have drunk and any food they might have eaten that night. Everything is suspect. Do I make myself clear?"

"Loud and clear, yes sir." Blake put the cake down and went out to the squad car and brought in the evidence kit, scooped the cake into one of the plastic bags, and labeled it. Johnston continued walking through the cottage. He looked at the paintings, many half-finished, that Jill had been working on. Not his style but he could tell she was, or had been, a talented artist. He walked into the living room and found the burnt plug attached to the mostly burnt hot plate. He picked up the plug and noticed that it looked like it had been tampered with, which would explain why the hot plate was destroyed. Odd, he thought, why would they have something like this laying around in their home? Seems like it should have been thrown out because it certainly couldn't be used or restored. It was trash.

"Ok, here's the cake. Anything else?"

"Yeah, take that hot plate and put that into evidence, too."

"But it looks like it was burnt in a fire. What does that have to do with two possible suicides?"

"I don't know, maybe nothing. But I have this feeling. When you've been doing this job as long as I have, you'll learn to listen to your gut more and more. And usually, it's right. Ok, let's get out of here."

Johnston stood outside the patrol car while Blake put the items from the house into the trunk. He couldn't stop staring up at the mansion, wondering if anyone had lived there, and what kind of people they'd been. The mansion was creepy, almost having a personality of its own. Whoever had lived there had to be creepy, too. Blake had said the place was empty. But he'd come back to double-check. If anyone lived there, maybe they'd know something. He would get to the bottom of it. He always did.

Chapter 18

Spring was in the air. The smells of grasses growing, flowers bursting through the wet leaf-covered dirt where snow was newly melted, the buds of new leaves pushing out of the tree branches, filled the air. The birds were returning to the area also and were looking for nesting materials, picking through the dead leaves from previous falls and any bits of sticks from dead trees that they could find. The cottage, also, once again had the sounds of life coming out of the windows. The chatter of a man and a woman could be heard through the open windows. The smell of fresh paint filled the air. There was music and laughter all around the cottage.

The invitation arrived in the mail.

Your presence is requested at the home of
Noah and Charlotte Charmein.
The occasion: Dinner and drinks
Date: Sunday, May 18
Time: 6:30pm
Dinner will be served promptly at 7pm
after drinks and hors d'oeuvres in the parlor.
Dessert and coffee will follow dinner
after a short rest in the parlor.
We request that you arrive on time.

♟ ♙

They arrived at the massive front doors to the mansion up the hill from where they were living. They stood in awe of the mansion for what seemed like twenty minutes but they knew couldn't have been more than a couple, both in their own worlds, admiring the stone work, the gardens near the front door, the overall architecture of the place that towered over their humble abode. They turned to each other and to the front door where they had just rung the door bell, waiting for a butler or some wait person to open the oversized solid double doors. When a gentleman in a smoking jacket and black trousers opened the door, they were sure it had to be Mr. Charmein himself.

"And you must be the Goldings, is it? Bob and Megan? I'm Noah, come into the parlor and you can meet my wife, Charlotte. We were just pouring some champagne."

Acknowledgements

As usual, I have my patient and extremely talented husband, Jim Fontaine, to thank for all the hard work he puts into all of my books to guarantee that they are the very best that they can be.

Thank you to all of my friends who support my work and everything that I write.

A special thank you to Donna Swett who gave me valuable feedback on my book. I appreciate the time and effort you took to read my book and provide me with exactly what I needed to fine tune a few rough passages that hopefully, made it a better read.

And thank you to NaNoWriMo (National Novel Writing Month) for being the catalyst for my writing the entire text of *Useful Pieces* in one month. Although it was written in 2019, sitting on the back burner for six years was exactly what I needed to prove to myself that it was a good story. And, as always, the editing process definitely improved the book you've just read.

About the Author

DJ Geribo, author and fine artist, lives in rural New Hampshire near Lake Winnipesaukee. After pursuing fine art for many years, she decided to focus on her writing and has completed several children's books, 'Eddie Easel and the Case of the Missing Green', 'Mouse Bound', and a middle-grade book, 'The House at the Top of the Trees'. She has also written a non-fiction book, 'The Miracle Dog', about one of her dogs that contracted a life-threatening disease. Her more recent books include a collection of literary short stories in 'Seven Storied Houses', and a collection of memories compiled from childhood events in 'Me and Them'. 'The Mart' combines a novel with a related collection of stories and 'Deep Lake House' introduces us to a variety of characters in individual stories that left a lasting impression on the House. 'Useful Pieces' is her ninth book.

Besides writing, which keeps DJ very busy, she also enjoys reading, of course, painting, exercise in many forms from lifting weights, e-bike riding, golfing in the summer with her husband, snowshoeing in the winter months, and walking any time of year. And she loves just hanging out with her Pomeranian and her Cockatoo.

DJ's books can be purchased at any of the following: the author's website at www.DJGeribo.com, BBD Publishing's website at www.BBDPublishing.com, and from Amazon where select titles are available in paperback and Kindle format. To learn about DJ's latest and forthcoming books, visit her website and join her e-mail list or visit BBD Publishing's website.

Other Books by DJ Geribo

Ten Storied Buildings: Author DJ Geribo's talent for telling stories continues to expand and Ten Storied Buildings, much like her Seven Storied Houses, clearly demonstrates why her tagline is "Writing gets real."
Softcover - $17.95

Deep Lake House: A collection of stories based on the people who've visited Deep Lake House over the span of a century. All of their stories have made a lasting impression on the House, the main character and narrator. Some sad, some uplifting and joyful, all likely to make an impression on the reader, too.
Softcover - $15.95

The Mart: A novel and collection of stories where the characters appear in both. Two main characters dominate the novel, while others have their starring roles in the individual stories. Together they complement each other in a world that can both break your heart and lift your spirits.
Softcover - $17.95

Me & Them: A memoir like none you've ever read before. If you grew up during the '50s and '60s, you'll feel right at home in this collection of vignettes on daily life. Some will make you laugh while others may make you cry. But you won't read this collection without reminiscing about your own childhood.
Softcover - $15.95

Seven Storied Houses: A house's facade isn't always a good indication of the kind of lives experienced by its occupants. A mansion doesn't mean a happy family any more than a much-in-need-of-repair home points to a life of misery. Both can be full of memories and only the occupants decide if they will be good or bad.
Softcover - $15.95

Mouse Bound: A story that came about after a mouse set up residence in the author's studio. After live-catching and driving the mouse to another location, she imagined the adventures he'd have experienced in returning to the best and only home he'd ever known, back in her studio.
Softcover - $10.95

The Miracle Dog: When the author's dog, Kameko, collapsed into her arms one summer morning, DJ knew something was very wrong. A trip to the vet confirmed a life-threatening diagnosis with DJ's precious Pomeranian spending nearly a week in an ICU at an emergency vet hospital that included four blood transfusions. After many daily trips back to the hospital, finally a combination of medicines saw DJ's beloved Pom back on the road to recovery.
Softcover - $16.95

Eddie Easel and the Case of the Missing Green: A creative children's story that teaches a child the basics of art and painting all through an engaging mystery. A story any child will love and one that may even start your child on an artistic career path.
Hardcover - $17.95 – Exclusively through BBD Publishing

The House at the Top of the Trees: While riding their bikes, Nat and Devon spot a house that appears to be sitting at the top of a tree. Curiously, they find a way to get there and discover a world unlike anything they've ever known before, a place where all of their dreams come true. Is it safe to stay or should they return home to their hard-working single mom who does her best to support her children who mean the world to her?
Softcover – $16.95

Coming Soon

The Castle at the Bottom of the Sea – the 2nd middle grade adventure book featuring Nat and Devon (from The House at the Top of the Trees) that takes them to the shore and another exciting and surreal adventure.

My Neighbor, the Alien – Jeff and his best friend Wilt are sure Jeff's neighbor is an alien. But what is he doing in their neighborhood? And how does he know their teacher from school? It seems the real learning has just begun for the two curious boys.

All of DJ's book can be purchased directly from www.BBDPublishing.com

You may also ask for her titles from your favorite bookseller.

Select titles can be purchased on Amazon in paperback and Kindle editions.

Leave Us a Review

Did you like *Useful Pieces*? BBD Publishing would love to hear your thoughts on this and any of the other books by author DJ Geribo that you've read.

Visit www.BBDPublishing.com and on the home page, click on the 'Submit A Comment' button in the right-hand column under the Readers' Comments. This will take you to the 'Submit Your Reader's Comments' form where you can share your comments about this or other books by DJ Geribo.

If you purchased this book on Amazon, please leave an Amazon Review to help other readers find and enjoy DJ's books.

Thank you for your interest in DJ Geribo's books.

www.ingramcontent.com/pod-product-compliance
Lightning Source LLC
Chambersburg PA
CBHW020516120726
47904CB00003B/860